MW01134181

Also by Jane O'Brien

The White Pine Trilogy

The Dunes & Don'ts
Antiques Emporium

The Kindred Spirit Bed & Breakfast

The Tangled Roots of Bent Pine Lodge

Jane O'Brien

The Tangled Roots of Bent Pine Lodge

Printed in the United States of America
Published by: Bay Leaf Publishing

Visit Jane O'Brien's Author page:
www.amazon.com/author/obrienjane

Visit her Blog:
www.authorjaneobrien.com

Contact her:

authorjaneobrien@gmail.com

This book is dedicated to my father, a decorated World War II veteran. He was in the 10th Armored Division, Company C, where he fought in Europe in three out of the four main battles, including the Battle of the Bulge. He passed away in 2011, and is sorely missed. He was a hero in the eyes of his family, as well as the United States government. Thanks for your service, Dad.

Table of Contents

A guiltie conscience is a worme that never ceaseth. Nicholas Ling

Politeuphuia, 1597

⌘ Chapter One ⌘

Kate - 2014

The gravel crunched under my tires as I turned onto the long drive through the woods that would take me to my parents' cottage. My car dipped and bobbed in the grooves made by the snow melt and runoff of the spring rains. The two-track should be graded and then smoothed out to a hard, dirt surface. It's one of many things I would have to take care of now that I had become the owner of the cottage in the woods.

I had forgotten what a long drive it was to get to the house. I haven't been here in several years. The thick oak and white pine forest formed a canopy overhead, creating a tunnel effect. The sun was blocked out completely, but I was familiar with the setting and felt very comfortable here. I knew what awaited me at the end of the quarter-mile stretch. And there it was, coming into view as I rounded the last curve. The sun was shining a welcoming ray, a beam that looked like it was meant just for this house, and this house only. It illuminated the opening around the large log cabin. It almost seemed as if a magical chord from the heavens should sound. For this was no ordinary log cabin. It was a work of art, created by my great-grandfather in the 1930s. It was built to last, and last it had, providing a sturdy home for my great-grandparents and my grandparents, as well, to raise their children in, and then later, when all the children were grown with families of their own, it was used as a family cottage for all to share until the day my parents retired and moved here permanently. They had not intended to be the sole owners, but as they liked to say, life happens. My mother's brother, Uncle Bill, passed away at an early age, never to have a wife or children. My mother's sister, Sarah, had moved to Iowa after marrying the love of her life. I was told there were several unsuccessful tries to get pregnant, but she remained childless. With the death of both of my grandparents, mother and father bought out Aunt Sarah's inherited share in the house. That's how we came to spend all of our summer vacations and many weekends through the year on the banks of the Muskegon River.

My sister, Lily, or Lillian as she preferred to be called now, was not interested in the house at all. She had become a very successful surgeon in Albuquerque, New Mexico, and since she never cared for the Michigan weather, she only came home when necessary. I had not seen her since our mother's funeral, and that was just fine with me. Recent events had made our already strained relationship now impossible to repair. The house had always belonged to the women in the family even though it emits a very rustic and masculine feel. Its ownership had passed from my great-grandparents, Wilhelm and Frances Bauer, to my grandparents, Sophia and Carl Klein, then my parents, Mary and Joe Lemanski, and now, after many stressful months, it belonged to me, Mary Katherine Lemanski, known to everyone simply as Kate. As I stopped the car near the front porch steps, the full weight of what that meant hit me. I had a lot to deal with, and I hoped I was up for the task.

I turned off the engine, rolled down the windows and just sat in my car for a moment, savoring the stillness. I had forgotten how quiet it was here without other people around. Usually, there were shouts of hellos with car doors slamming as the newest arrivals carried in baskets of food, suitcases, and games for the kids. The activity would send all wildlife away, deep into the trees. But, today, I was able to listen to what it must be like when no one is around. The bird calls were so loud it would be incorrect to call this place a quiet sanctuary. The birds seemed to be announcing to all that spring had finally arrived. The next thing I noticed was the familiar sound of rushing water, as the Muskegon River raced past the lodge, always a danger to us kids when we were small, and a constant worry to my mother. "Don't go near the water," she would call out. I can almost hear her voice now, and I miss it so.

I opened the car door and stepped out onto a bed of dried pine needles. Was there anything else that smelled as good? For me, the fragrance of a burning applewood fire in the fireplace was like sweet candy and was its equal. It filled my nostrils with a lovely sensation as I inhaled deeply, and I almost cried as I realized that I was finally here, exactly where I wanted to be.

I had been paying a local handyman to check in on the place now and then, making sure there were no break-ins, roof leaks, or bursting pipes. He must have anticipated my arrival today and had started a welcoming fire. I will have to thank him for the gesture, and reminded myself it was time to take back my spare key. My key – I liked the sound of that.

I walked hesitantly up the steps to the wrap-around porch. The steps were firm and well-maintained. Nothing to worry about there. The porch was solid, as well. I was glad for that. I did not relish the idea of having to dig right in to heavy-duty repairs. I had a bigger job ahead of me. I turned the key to the door and stepped across the threshold. This was the first time I have gone through the door since my mother's funeral three years ago, and without a parent to greet me, it was a strange sensation. The house seemed devoid of spirit. I had always felt that a house retains something of the past owners, so if a family had been happy there, it should be felt in the air, and for the most part we had been, but on the day of my mother's funeral, my sister and I had had a terrible fight, leaving some very bad vibes in our wake. I planned on changing that by working hard to make this empty log house my home, with everything that entailed.

Each time a new person came to visit here for the first time, you could literally hear their intake of breath. At first they'd see only the entry with its log walls and paneled ceiling. The hardwood floors were usually buffed to a soft sheen. My mother was a spotless housekeeper; nothing was ever overlooked. And then the guest would be invited into the main room, known as the great room. Exposed ends of some logs showed the diameter of the hand-hewn Douglas fir to be about 18 inches. The ceilings here reached up to 20 feet, with huge beams seemingly holding it all up. Then all eyes would go to the massive fireplace, made by my great-grandfather's own hands as he placed fieldstones, one at a time, along one wall and all the way up to the ceiling's peak. A large log which had been flattened on the top served as the mantle which my mother always decorated according to the season. You would think all of the wood would make the interior dark and dreary, but instead the light pine color had a glowing effect, especially when a fire danced in the hearth, casting shadows and light on the walls.

I noticed the bulky leather sofa and chairs were still covered with sheets, and there was plenty of dusting to do, but overall I was quite pleased with what I had come home to.

I couldn't wait to get started on my new life here in the woods of Western Michigan. First though, I had a lot to carry in. I had tried not to bring too much, because I knew the house was completely furnished, but I had stopped at the grocery store on the way here so I could stock up the cupboards. In and out of the car, up and down the steps, and I had finally hauled it all in. I stood in the kitchen, glancing around; it was a little disconcerting being here all by myself. That was another thing I would have to adjust to.

My father always kept an old record player on a stand with a shelf full of 78 and 33 RPM records. He claimed to love that sound better than the quality of a CD. He said the scratches added character and realness that modern technology didn't convey. I searched through the record jackets until I found one of his favorites, clicked on the turntable, and lowered the needle. There it was – I could feel the spirit of the house returning. Happy times filled the air. I could almost hear my father singing and see him spinning my mother around as she laughingly sang along. My sister and I were trying to imitate what they were doing, giggling as we tripped over our own feet. The song was Up A Lazy River, which was not really my parents' era but rather my grandparents'. Grandpa was a singer, too, and had taught us the words to the song while we bounced on his knee. Now that I sensed happiness again, I could open the bottle of Fenn Valley Pinot Grigio I had brought along to celebrate my arrival. I grabbed a glass from the cupboard, threw back the sheet on the sofa, kicked off my shoes, lit a candle which had been left on the coffee table, and sat back with a sigh, ready to enjoy the fire. Yes, this is for real. I had really done it. I had changed the direction of my life and accomplished one of my goals – moving back to where things were simple and I was happy.

⌘ Chapter Two ⌘

Conor ~ 2011

I walked slowly around my house in a daze. It had been six months already since Tammy's funeral. I didn't remember much about it, except that people were always coming up to me and saying "Sorry for your loss, if I can do anything, give me a call." I was sure they all meant well, and someday I knew I would look back on it all and I'd know how much they all cared. But right now the pain was so severe I could hardly breathe. I couldn't eat or sleep, either. Whenever I closed my eyes, all I saw was her laughing eyes, and those sensual lips that were just begging to be kissed. I was drawn to her the minute I laid eyes on her. She was walking down the hall in high school, carrying her books in front of her. I watched her glide gracefully along with a gentle sway of her hips. She wasn't aware of it, and certainly didn't use it to gain attention, but she had a unique way of moving. Each foot would be gently placed before the next one hit the ground, in the way an Indian might walk through the woods without breaking a twig. The way she held her books reminded me of a Potowatomie woman carrying the wood she had found for her fire, with ease and confidence, knowing that she had done well for her family. I later discovered that Tammy was a ballet dancer, which explained her grace and gentleness.

I didn't remember when the last time was that I had taken a shower. Some things I did automatically, like making the morning coffee (always my job) and some things I didn't do at all, like drinking it. There was a heavy weight on my chest, and I wanted nothing more than to sleep in a dark room all day and all night just to make it all go away. My beautiful Tammy was gone! My angel. My life! How could that possibly be? I couldn't imagine my world without her in it anymore

They told me that she had not suffered and death had been instant, as if that would make it better. Didn't they understand that nothing could make it better? I wished with every fiber of my body that I had been in that car with her. Maybe I could have yelled "Deer!" and she would have been able to swerve in time to avoid the stupid beast! Maybe I would have been driving and I would have been the one who was killed -- that would have been fine with me. Or maybe, just maybe, we both would have died, and we would be together in Heaven right now, or wherever you go when life has come to an end. At this point I was not so sure that God even existed, because if he did how could he be so cruel? How could he take her and leave me behind?

I've thought many times about joining her. It would be so easy. There are many ways a person could take their own life – guns, pills, running my car into a tree, or letting the car run in the garage. That last one would be the easiest. There would be nothing for anyone to clean up and I could just go to sleep and never wake up again here on Earth. Maybe I would find myself in my Tammy's arms in Heaven, because if there is one, that's where my sweet angel is, but then Pop and Ellen would be suffering the same pain I am now and I could never let that happen. When Mom died, I was only ten. I watched my father go through what I was dealing with now, but as a kid I was so wrapped up in my own misery I couldn't understand his. Pop used the bottle to numb his pain, and Ellen and I were left alone to figure things out for ourselves. I took care of her, and got her off to school. I was the one who made our lunches and placed hers carefully in a clean Mork and Mindy lunchbox, I was the one who had to find us a snack after school, and most times, I was the one who tucked her into bed at night and assured her that I would always take care of her, no matter what. Pop was good at hiding his drinking, and Ellen and I were good at hiding how it was at home for us. If I had been a little older and a little smarter, I would have asked for help, but for some reason we thought it was shameful the way he was, and we didn't want anyone to find out, so we covered. And now here I was, heading in that same direction, but I didn't care because there was no one to answer to. I had been denied my right to become a father to Tammy's babies, our babies, the babies we dreamed of having someday.

I had had a bottle of whiskey in the cupboard; it had been there for a year or more, because I rarely drank hard alcohol; I had always been afraid of the "Irish curse" and I didn't want to be like Pop, but then again I never knew my life might follow the same path as his, losing his wife at a young age. And no one seemed to notice so far. I had learned from the best how to hide my drinking, so I guess they all thought my red-rimmed, puffy eyes were from crying. There had been plenty of that, too, so it wasn't hard to convince them. I had a bucket that I carried around with me, to catch the vomit that came on me unexpectedly, whenever I thought of Tammy in the car on the side of the road, with no one to hold her as she breathed her last breath. The only way to get rid of that image was to drink more until I couldn't see the picture in my head anymore, until the blackness came and I was put out of my misery. And that's exactly what happened the day that Ellen discovered me blacked out in the hammock in the yard.

"Conor, wake up! Conor, can you hear me?" I woke up to Ellen's voice, calling me over and over again. She was in a panic, she had never seen me drink to excess, but God knows I had plenty of reason. She shook me over and over and I was having trouble coming to. I couldn't get my eyes to focus. I opened my eyes a little more, shook my head, and then lost my guts over the side of the hammock.

"Sorry, Ellen, I must have had something bad to eat last night."

"Don't you pull that crap with me, Conor McAuley! I was right there with you when we went through all of this with Pop. You will not take me down that road again!" And with that she gave him a punch in the shoulder.

"Ow! What did I do deserve that? I'm just sick, I promise," said Conor, still thinking he could fake his drunk.

"Come on, Conor, let's get you into the house and in the shower. You stink! And shave off some of the scruff growing on your face! It might look sexy on some men, but on you it's just plain disgusting." Ellen pulled on my arm, until I had no choice but to sit up and follow her. I really was quite embarrassed with the fact that she had found me like this. Ellen pushed me into the house and down the hall to the bathroom. She grabbed some fresh towels from the linen closet and shoved them in my hands. It was the last of the towels.

"My word, Conor, it looks like I am going to have to do your laundry today while I'm here. Now, get in there, and get rid of your filth, and don't come out until you're squeaky clean." I glared at her, giving her my big brother stare, but then I did what she demanded. Funny how the tables were turned and she was now taking care of me. It had always been my role to watch over her. Maybe she was right and there was a better way to try to handle this misery than with the bottle. I suddenly realized that the last thing I wanted was to put Ellen through the

Hell we had gone through as kids. We both loved Pop to death because once he came out of it, he had been the best dad in the world. He had been trying to make up for that period of time, when he was in a dark hole, ever since. It seemed like a lot of trouble spending the rest of your life making up for your mistakes.

While the hot water beat on my head and face, I cried, freely, letting the tears merge with the water as it washed down my body, knowing full well that Ellen couldn't hear me over the noise of the shower. I cried for the loss of my wife, and I cried for the fact that Ellen had made me realize that I had to make every effort to start anew, which meant that I would not be able to think about Tammy every waking minute. I would have to let a small part of her go, because, otherwise, it would be impossible to get through an entire workday without showing my emotion to others. There would be times when I would have to suppress my feelings in order to function, for the sake of others. I couldn't stand the look of pity in their eyes, or the whispers behind my back, I had become used to the depression and I rather liked it. It fit me like a glove and, in my mind, it proved to me how much I still loved Tammy. Not thinking about her even for a few minutes of the day was unthinkable. I worked out a plan while I was soaping up and letting the hot water scorch my body – I would only drink a little when I was home, just enough to take the edge off. I would switch to vodka so no one could smell it on my breath, and maybe if they thought I was getting better, they would leave me alone.

I stepped out of the shower, toweled my hair dry, wrapped a big towel around my waist, and intended to grab some fresh clothes out of my bedroom – our bedroom, the bedroom where only one half of the bed was ever warm now, the bedroom that was slowly losing the smell of her. As I stepped onto the carpet, from the cold tile of the bathroom, I almost tripped over a clean pair of jeans and a fresh tee shirt Ellen had left outside the door. I had to admit that I did feel a little better, some of the darkness had disappeared – but only some. I didn't expect it would ever go away. How could it? Tammy had left a big whole in my heart that could never be filled, and I knew I would never be the same man again.

⌘ Chapter Three ⌘

Lily -1986

It was the first day of junior high – seventh grade. We would be attending a brand new building and so that made it that much more exciting. It didn't seem to matter that none of us knew where we were going; we wouldn't look like fools to the older kids when we were lost, since they were in the same boat. Everyone was walking around with their schedule in their hands and dazed expressions on their faces, looking for their homerooms. For me, the first day of school was always the most thrilling. We wondered who we would get for teachers. Who would be in our classes? Would we meet any cute new boys? But most of all would they notice that Lillian Lemanski is the most beautiful girl in school? I already knew there would not be any competition in that area. My sister, Kate, was pretty, but she couldn't hold a candle to me. I could see it each and every time I looked in the mirror. I had been aware of my beauty since I was a baby.

This year, I planned to not only keep current on fashion trends, but I also would work on my grades, so I could stay on the honor roll. The honor roll had never been available to me until now, and even though I wasn't quite sure what it entailed, I knew I had to be at the top of my class. I always wanted to be at the top of everything I did. I loved to win more than anything. Each Christmas we would get some new games for the family to play over winter break, and every year I would challenge Kate to one of the board games. I always won, because, for me, losing was not an option -- not to anyone, especially not to Kate.

Everyone was noisily chattering in the halls, as they walked together in groups. For most of them, I guess being in a group of two or more made them feel safe, but being alone had never bothered me. At home I had Kate, of course, but I didn't need her at my side for every little thing. Kate tended to be a little clingy. She seemed to need me more than I needed her. I would have been perfectly happy if Mama and Papa had only had one child. I don't think I would have missed my sibling one bit. I was glad that we would not be in any of the same classes together. I never like being compared to her. It was insulting. Kate on the other hand always thanked everyone so politely for the compliment. Having a sister with the same hair and eye color was difficult. I tried to be different from her by changing my hair style often, but she would always say, "that's cute, Lily." and then she would go and get hers done the same way. I was hoping I would be able to keep my distance this year. Maybe since we were in different classes, we would be moving in different circles. I was sure my friends would not want her tagging along, anyway. I didn't have any friends yet, just the kids I knew from grade school, but I planned on ditching them as soon as I found out who the "cool" kids were.

I walked into my homeroom and took a seat towards the middle of the classroom. I never wanted to be in view of the teacher if I could help it, but I knew that sitting too far back was for losers. A good-looking boy with blonde hair and dimples smiled at me, so I knew I was off to a good start. He leaned over and said, "Hi, I'm Mark Sanders. How do you like it so far?"

"Well, I haven't seen anything yet but crowded halls, but I'm sure I'll adjust just fine; I'm very adaptable. And my name is Lily, by the way." I offered him my best smile, and look at him through my eyelashes so he could get the best effect. That tactic had worked well before; I knew I had him already. He was cute so he would do until I could size up the territory. Then if need be, I could toss him without a moment's notice.

"What class do you have for first period?" he asked.

I glanced down at the schedule in my hand and said, "It looks like I start the day with American

History with Mr. Davis. Sounds like a boring beginning."

"Hey, me too," Mark said. "Can I walk with you to class?"

"Sure, why not. We can find it together." And that was how it went throughout the rest of the day. In each class, I found a boy that was willing to be my friend, and would walk me down the halls, showing everyone that saw me, that I was special and someone they would want to be friends with. And in that short amount of time, I had figured out the game that can be found in all schools that is called "popularity."

The hours just flew by, as I built up my posse, and learned my way around the building, and soon sixth period was over. I met Kate by the main entrance, just like we had previously arranged, so we could ride home together when Mama came to pick us up.

"Hey, Lily, did you have a good day?" asked Kate filled with interest.

"Yes, I did actually," I said, "I met a lot of new people and made them all my best friends."

Kate laughed. "Oh, Lily, they can't all be best friends. The word "best" is superlative, so you can only have one best friend."

"Kate, you always think you're so smart with your grammar and spelling, but I know one thing better than you. Make them all best friends and they'll do anything you say."

"But why do you need to control people like that? The kids will catch on soon enough, and then no one will like you."

"Not if you stay ahead of the game. I can never let my guard down. I have big plans to be homecoming queen when I get into high school, and it takes years to build a reputation. You can never start too early." Just then Mama pulled up and we hopped into the car.

"How was your first day at Harper Junior High, girls?" asked Mama, looking over the back seat with a big smile.

"It was great," we both said in unison.

"Well, let's get you home so I can hear all about it. I want every last detail."

That was one thing about Mama that I loved. She always gave us her undivided attention after school. She loved hearing the stories of our day. But how I wished she would learn to dress a little better like the other moms did. She didn't care to spend her money on name brand clothing. She said it wasn't necessary; that we could find cute clothes in pretty colors in the discount stores. Mama felt it wasn't necessary to show off a label. Kate always seemed to agree with her, but I knew that you wouldn't get any friends in school unless you knew how to dress. One day soon, when I graduated from college, I would make a lot of money, and then I could buy anything I wanted. If Kate and Mama and Papa didn't want to keep up with me, then I would leave them behind in my dust. They'd see, I was going to be somebody, no matter what, and I wouldn't let anything or anybody get in my way.

⌘ Chapter Four ⌘

Kate - 2014

The bright morning light attacked my slumber. I was glad the chalet-style windows were on the west side of the lodge. Great-grandpa loved a good evening sunset, I was told, so at least the sun wasn't beaming in my eyes. I'll have to deal with that only on the rare occasion when I go to bed early and the sun is setting, and since I don't usually need a lot of sleep, that wouldn't be happening anytime soon. Now something else was assaulting my senses. My cell phone was ringing, but I had no idea where I had left it. I jumped out of bed, ran down the loft steps and into the kitchen. I found it on the counter with the mess of bread, crackers, and other dry goods I had not put away yet. I hoped my mother was not looking down on me this morning. I quickly grabbed the phone.

"Hello?" I said in my raspy morning voice.

"Thank God, you're alive!" Cara, my best

friend in Chicago, was prone to drama. "I tried calling several times last night to see if you had made it okay, but I couldn't get through."

"I'm fine, Miss Worrywart! Cell service is spotty here. I have to be right here in the kitchen or on the porch in order to get bars. I'll text you the landline number; then you can reach me anytime I'm home. Sometimes texting goes through when a call doesn't, so you can try that, too."

Cara let out a big sigh. "I still don't understand why you wanted to turn your life upside down, giving up a great career, for living in the woods in Michigan."

"You of all people should get it, Cara," I said. "You were there for the worst time in my life. I don't know how I would have made it without you."

"And that's exactly where I wanted to be," she said.

"I really do know why you needed a change, but Michigan? What is there to do there? Are there any good coffee shops, or libraries? And what about the theater? Oh, my goodness, where will you buy quality wine?"

"Cara, calm down," I said. "We talked about this already. I might be in the woods, but I'm not away from civilization. My driveway is only a quarter-mile long, and then I'm right back out on the highway. What is it about people who live in a big city? They always seem to think the rest of the country is living like pioneers."

"Okay, I get it. But I'm going to miss you so much," she said.

"You'll come to visit. Chicago is only a few hours away."

"I'll give it a try when I know there is no more possibility of snow. I've had enough this year right where I am, and I know your area will get plenty long after we are through seeing any."

"Well, that's not really true," I explained patiently. "We are far enough inland here so we don't always get lake-effect snow like they do along the shoreline. And you're in the Windy City; we don't have arctic blasts like you do there. You'd like it here, I'm sure of it." Though I wasn't really sure of it, at all. Cara was a died-in-the-wool city girl. That's all she had ever known. Getting used to birds, bears, and coyotes might be a terrifying idea to her.

"Well, I just wanted to make sure you were safe. You don't have anyone to check up on you anymore, so I'm officially taking on that role. So, how was it sleeping alone in the house? Were you afraid?"

"Not at all," I lied. "I had a great night's sleep. But I admit it is a little lonely with no one to talk to." And no one to watch out for the "bogeyman," but I would never let Cara know that. I'm a grown woman. I can handle being alone just fine, I think.

I have known Cara since my first day of work at a small library in a Chicago suburb. I was green, fresh out of college, trained in family history research, and ready to start my new career as a genealogy librarian. Cara had already been there for a year, so she took me under her wing. We shared coffee breaks and lunches and soon became fast friends. Our work station desks were next to each other, so we often did a little gossiping when no one was looking. I've loved libraries since I was young girl and first learned to read; I've often visited libraries in cities I'm traveling through just to see their setup and the way they display new books. There's something very special about handling a book and even smelling the print. I have to admit to loving my new e-reader, but I'm afraid, with new technology being updated all the time, that libraries will someday be extinct and the thought of that makes me sad.

After a few months of working together, Cara and I had become so close that we decided to become roommates and share expenses. That was a great help with my entry level salary. We got along very well and still do to this day, although Cara is a mother hen and seems to consider me one of her chicks, but I have to admit to appreciating the fact that I am important to at least one person on this planet.

"– and so we had drinks and then went home. The date wasn't much to write home about, that's for sure. Kate? Are you still there?" Cara asked.

Apparently, I had zoned out a bit, as I often do when she goes on one of her rambling conversations.

"Sure, sure, I'm here," I said, faking my lack of attention. "That's too bad that he wasn't the guy for you. Someone will come along soon; they can't all be jerks, right?"

I glanced at the clock and realized that my morning was slipping away. "Look, Cara, I'd love to talk more, but I got in later than I planned yesterday, and I still have unpacking to do and a lot of cleaning to take care of before I can feel comfortable here. So, please forgive me, but I should get going. I'll call later tonight, and we can have a long chat over a glass of wine."

"That's fine," she said. "I understand. I need to get to work anyway. I'll tell the girls you're doing fine and you said hello. Take care." And with that she hung up and I was once again standing in silence, a very weird and strange sensation for me still.

I just turned and headed for the stairs to the loft bathroom for my morning shower, when someone knocked at the door. Shoot, who could that be at this hour? I was still in my flannel pajama bottoms and had thrown an old ragged hoodie over my tank top when I came downstairs. My feet were bare and were by now getting quite cold on the hardwood floor. I'd been fussing with my hair while talking to Cara, just to get it off my neck and I had managed to get it in a sort of rat's nest pony tail. Well, I'd better see who it was; it must be important to come calling at 8:00 a.m. on a Saturday!

I approached the door realizing that I really should have some sort of peep hole. Another thing to put on the to-do list. Opening the door to a stranger wasn't safe so far off the road in these dense woods, but today I had no choice. I put on a happy face, better to throw the "bad guy" off, swung back the door, and lost my balance. I came close to landing on my derriere, but I was able to hang onto the doorknob for stability and then I righted myself. Not a very graceful way to meet a new neighbor. As I looked up, I saw a pair of blue eyes that almost made me lose my balance again. How could anyone's eyes be that blue? Colored contacts? Pretty vain for a man. He was dressed in jeans and a plaid flannel shirt; but then what else would I expect him to be wearing in the North? He was about my age, approximately 5'10", dark hair, and a slight cleft in the chin. A ruggedly handsome man, but not a perfect face. I noticed a small scar above his right eyebrow and another near his chin -- a thin line that ran right along the jawbone. I took all of this in, in a millisecond, while trying to regain my grace. I might need this description for the police later if this turned out to be a "bad guy." There was something distinctly familiar about him, but I couldn't place it.

"Good morning," he said. His voice had a deep timbre and was very easy to listen to; like soft velvet caressing my ears. "I hope I didn't wake you. I just wanted to see how you managed on your first night, so I came by to return the spare key. My name is Conor McAuley; I've been watching your place for you." He extended his hand, and I felt a jolt of electricity at his touch. I thought he felt it, too, by the surprised look in his eyes.

"Come in, Mr. McAuley. I'm Mary Katherine,

but everyone calls me Kate. I'm sorry. I'm in a bit of a mess. I haven't had time to unpack and clean up yet." I was still a little nervous, but I thought inviting him in was the neighborly thing to do.

"Please, call me Conor. It's nice to meet you," he said. "I've been anxious to see who the newest owner is. I've loved this place since I was a kid."

"I'm sorry, but I thought you were older. I was told you were an old friend of my father's," I said, a little confused.

"That would be my father, Eric McAuley. He's been under the weather lately, so I've been taking care of things for him. We live on the property adjoining yours. There's actually a path that you can take right through the woods to my place, although it's quite a hike. We have 40 acres and I guess that's about the size of your plot, too. So you really can't see my house from here."

Now that I knew the story, I felt obliged to be a good neighbor. "Do you have time for coffee?" I asked. "I was just about to make a pot. It's a nice fresh bag of gourmet grounds – hasn't even been opened yet."

"Thank you, but I really shouldn't stay. I have a job to get to. It's been tough doing my work and Dad's, too. I always seem to be behind schedule. I just wanted to ask if the furnace kicked on okay. I'm not sure how much longer it's going to last. I've cleaned the contacts and filter, but it still seems to be a bit fussy. I was hoping it would come on for you. There's quite a chill in the air this morning, but it should warm up in a bit."

"Oh, yes. It's fine," I said. "The house was toasty this morning. And where are my manners? I forgot to thank you for making the fire yesterday. It was so nice to come home to. You've done a great job here. Please send me your bill, so I can take care of it right away. I really appreciate all you've done."

"No problem, at all," he said with a quick glance around. "It gave me a chance to see the interior. I'm a big fan of log homes. The craftsmanship here is some of the best I've seen," he said as his eyes rested on the fireplace. "Well, I should be on my way. Call if you need anything at all." A slight smile curved his lips as he said, "And, again, nice to see you." An odd choice of words, I thought. Isn't that phrase usually reserved for people you've met before? I watched as his eyes scanned my body from bottom to top, then he turned and went down the steps to his Jeep Cherokee and drove off.

After he left and I had closed the door, I decided I might as well get the coffee started. I had brought a new Ethiopian, organic, fair-trade bean that I was looking forward to trying. On my way to the kitchen, I glanced in the hall mirror that mother always kept for a last minute check before going out the door. Oh, no! No wonder he had said, "It was nice to 'see' you." My sweatshirt had slipped off my shoulder and was hanging open at the front, revealing the fact that I wore nothing underneath but a thin tank top, a very thin tank top. I felt my cheeks burn. Oh well, there's nothing there I'm sure he hasn't seen before. Of course, he hasn't seen mine before! So much for making a good impression with my first new acquaintance here. He probably thinks of me as a "wild" big city woman who is totally uninhibited! I can't do a thing about that now; I probably won't be seeing him anytime soon, anyway.

Okay, off to the shower and then I could get my morning started. I put on the pot of coffee to brew while I was getting ready to go out. There was a lot I wanted to accomplish today, but I had decided there was no rush; I would not put pressure on myself to meet some unrealistic deadline of my own making. Anyway, it was just my obsessive behavior that was driving me. I have been like this since I was a child; once I get an idea in my head, I can't stop until I solve it or complete the job. While drifting off to sleep last night, I had made a decision to move a little slower and start enjoying life. I wanted to be more like the locals, becoming one with nature, and appreciating the many wonders of my surroundings.

After a quick shower and my satisfying cup of coffee, I stepped into my jeans and pulled on a Maize and Blue U of M sweatshirt, and then I checked my auburn hair in the mirror. I was pleased with the look of the new haircut I had gotten before coming here. The smooth swing of the shoulder-cut gave me a carefree look that went perfectly with the minimum amount of makeup I would be wearing from here on. I automatically leaned in closer to inspect my eyeliner and mascara, looking straight into my hazel eyes before realizing, with the new clean look, this was no longer necessary. I grabbed my purse, cell phone, and keys, and made a stop at the door to put on my new L.L. Bean hiking boots. Before I came here I did a little shopping online and when I spotted these boots, I knew I had to have them. They're a beautiful rustic red color (which I'm sure will get more rustic as I walk the property) and they're just right for the mood I was in. Happy for the first time in a very long time. Would anyone notice that I had red boots on with a blue and yellow sweatshirt? Not at all. I had spent enough time here growing up to know that those things were just not important. Chicago-style fashion would be laughed out of the county, anyway.

Heading down my bumpy driveway, I again made a mental note to contact someone about smoothing it out. In fact, I needed to make a list of everything that has to be done and then prioritize it. That's my M.O. That's the way I get through life. Lists. But my first stop was not on any list, and before I arrived in River County it was the farthest thing on my mind. Last night while sitting in front of the fire with my glass of wine, I was thinking of all the little things in life I had missed out on and how I would go about changing that. And the number one thing I had always wanted and never had was a dog of my own. Although I wasn't afraid of being here alone, not really, it was very quiet, almost too quiet. There was no one to talk to, and although I don't talk quite as much as Cara, sometimes words just have to come out. I know a dog can't talk back, but at least he can listen, or at least look like he's listening. So now I was heading out to find the nearest dog shelter. I'd like to get a rescue dog, but I haven't the faintest idea what size or breed to look for. As I came to the end of the drive, I turned right onto the highway and turned south towards town.

I knew the county buildings were beyond the village, and I was sure I had seen a sign for a dog shelter there. On the way, I passed the library. My head automatically turned to check it out. It was a newly renovated building and looked very promising. I couldn't wait to get inside, but that would have to wait for another day. I slowed down as I came to a grouping of buildings that included the County Sheriff's office. Yes, there it was – River County Dog Shelter. Okay, here it goes. Let's see what, or who, they had to offer. I had told myself not to fall for the first dog I saw. Take my time. Be patient. Maybe today isn't the right day, and I will have to come back another time.

As I opened the door, I almost wanted to cover my ears. The many different pitches of excited barking was deafening as it echoed around the interior. There were even some howls that almost seemed mournful. I instantly had the feeling of wanting to save them all. I hoped I could limit myself to just one furry friend. There was no one behind the counter, and I wasn't quite sure what to do with myself so I wandered over to the bulletin board and read a few hints on how to care for a pet, and lightly scanned some fliers of upcoming events in the area. Finally, a door creaked and then slammed heavily, and I heard a friendly voice say, "Is there something I can do for you?"

"Hi," I said, putting my hand out, "I'm interested in finding a dog for a companion. It sounds like you have quite a selection back there."

"We sure do. I'm sorry about all of the racket. I was just feeding them and once they see the first dog getting food, they get a little excited," she said with a pleasant giggle. "What type of dog are you looking for? Small, medium, large? Shedding or non? Herder, hunter, or lap dog? We have quite a variety here today. It's too bad there are so many waiting for good homes. River County is a no-kill shelter, so some of these guys have been here for quite a while."

I thought about that for a second and then said, "I guess I'm looking for a medium to large dog. I want a companion, one that I can wrap my arms around and love. I have plenty of room for a dog to run; I live on 40 acres by the river. I like to hike, so

I'd like a dog that can walk along with me through the woods. But I'm pretty sure I don't want a puppy, because I don't think I'm up for the housebreaking routine. Owning a dog is a new thing for me, and I don't think I'd know how to deal with a puppy."

"Okay," she said. "Now we're getting somewhere. I have ideas for you, but first you'll have to fill out the required forms. You'll be expected to pay for all shots and the license. And if you select a dog that has not been neutered or spayed yet, we would do that here for you before you are able to take the dog home, but you'll have to pay for that also. So if that sounds acceptable, we can get started."

"Yes, let's do it. I'm ready and excited."

"Okay. Here's a clipboard. You can take a seat over there, and when you are done filling it out, we'll take a walk out back."

After filling out several forms and answering questions about my entire life story, it seemed, I was ready to select my new "best friend." I entered a large warehouse-type setting. There were small to large individual cages, some housing dogs that were sleeping or maybe not feeling well. Then there were three large basketball-court sized fenced-in areas with slides, balls, and kiddy pools.

"Each one of these yards are designated by size of the dogs," said the dog shelter employee. "We don't let the little Chihuahuas play with the Saint Bernards. We're here to save the dogs, not hurt them more. All dogs have to be socialized before they can play with the others; that's why some are still in individual cages. They're the ones that have not been around other dogs enough to know how to behave. We'll work with them a little each day until they become used to the routine, and they'll soon learn to enjoy playtime. But for you, never having owned a dog before, I think you should look for something that already has had some training."

"Oh, I agree with you 100%," I said as I looked through the fencing. There was a variety of what appeared to be mixed breeds and a few breeds that were recognizable to me. Most of the dogs instantly came over to the fence to check me out, most likely looking for treats.

"Is it okay to put my hand close to the fencing so they can smell me? I've read that is a good thing to do."

"Oh, sure. Every one of these guys in here is a lover. It's safe. So if this is the size you are looking for it's now up to you. Well, to be more precise," she said, "it's probably one of them that will do the choosing."

"What do you mean?" I asked.

"You'll see," she said with that giggle again. "Just give it some time."

About 15 dogs were nuzzling me through the fencing, each one wanting to be touched and to see if my hands revealed what I had last had to eat. My eyes were drawn to one particular large white dog. The eyes seemed sad, but also intelligent and very inquisitive. As some of the others lost interest and moved away to continue in their play, he stayed behind, quietly sitting and patiently waiting for something.

"This dog is a purebred yellow lab. He does not have a chip and had no collar when we found him. His picture and information have been in the local paper, because we were hoping the owner would come forward. Since this is a tourist area, and a hunting/fishing area as well, we often find dogs that were lost by their traveling owners. Sometimes they are separated from their dogs in the woods and they are forced to leave them behind. A few have jumped from the car or the back end of a truck at a gas station stop and the owners never notice until it's too late. Unfortunately, on occasion, they are purposely left behind with no collar or tags so their original owners will not be called. Would you like me to let him out?" she asked.

"Oh yes. I need to meet this one. You said he's a yellow lab; I've seen them before, but he is so white."

"Very light colored labs which look white are still considered to be yellow Labrador retrievers. Breeders often strive to get the whitest color possible," she said, stroking his head through the fencing. "I'm sure he was a very expensive dog. It's truly a shame if someone lost him, but they should have had the chip put in. Then we would have known who he belonged to, and we could have notified them that he was here. It's something you might want to consider if you take him."

She opened the gate and was careful that he was the only one to pass through. He instantly came to me. He was not aggressive at all, but seemed more inquisitive than anything else. I had prepared myself for a jump up to my shoulders with large paws on my chest, but he just quietly nudged at my knees. I squatted down next to him and let him sniff my hair and face. I ran my hands all over his body. His coat was thick and slightly rough, but when I touched his ears, it was like touching velvet. I felt no fear from this stranger whatsoever. Then he did the most amazing thing. He laid down next to me and put his head on my feet, and sighed.

"There it is," she said with a broad grin.

"What?"

"You've just been chosen!"

"I have?" I asked. "But what made him want me?"

"That will be between you and him for the rest of your life, if you take him home. But, for whatever reason, he's already decided to assign himself as your protector and companion. And the good part is that he is already neutered and his shots are up-to-date. He's been here for the required waiting period, so if you like him, he can go home with you today."

"Oh, wow. That's quick," I said feeling somewhat overwhelmed. "Is that really all there is to it?"

"Well, we do have to see your driver's license, and get you put into our system for the county records. But other than that, he's all yours."

"I truly love him. But I have a few questions, about food, etc. Oh, and does he already have a name?"

"He surely does. We name all of the dogs as they come in, if they don't have any tags. This is Hoagie. H-O-A-G-I-E."

"Hoagie?"

She saw the shocked look on my face and thought I needed an explanation. "One of our employees is from New Jersey. We have a running joke about the name of our sandwiches, which we call submarines here, or just plain subs. She is insistent that they are hoagies and refuses to call them subs. So when it was her turn to pick a name, she chose Hoagie. You looked so surprised when I said his name. Any particular reason?"

"Yes," I said trying to contain my joy, "I've just been given a sign. Hoagy Carmichael, spelled with a 'y' was the writer and original performer of a song in 1930 called Up a Lazy River. It's a family favorite. I've just been shown that my grandpa is looking down on me and approves this selection.

"Hoagy, let's go home." And with that, my gentle white beast jumped up and let out a happy bark. I had just acquired my first River County friend.

⌘ Chapter Five ⌘

Kate - 2014

I was on my way home with Hoagy in the back seat. The dog shelter had provided a leash and collar – I'm sure I must have paid for it in all the other fees that were required. I had no idea my impulsive decision to own a dog would take such a bite out of my wallet. At this point in my life, money was not an issue, but soon I would have to start watching my pennies and get a job. Right now, though, I was enjoying the time off that I had given myself to just relax and become me again. I hoped Hoagy would be a part of that journey.

As soon as I opened the car door, he hopped right in, perfectly at ease with the routine. It was obvious he'd done this before. I decided to stop at the farm store on the way home to pick up a few more things he would need to feel at home; toys, bowls, a bed, food, and snacks. I left him in the car and he watched anxiously as I walked away, already attached to my every move. It didn't take long to rack up another large bill, wheel the cart out to the car, and load up, and then we were on our way.

When we arrived, I cautiously opened the back car door and reached in the driver's side for the leash which I had kept connected to his collar. I was unsure how he would react to freedom after being in an enclosed space, and I didn't want to risk him running off. Hoagy was very co-operative, though, and after a short visit to a nearby tree where he lifted his leg and got some relief, we walked right in the house. As soon as I unhooked the leash, he did a quick exploration of his new surroundings, sniffing at every object he could reach, and then he sat at my feet. This, I discovered, was now what he thought of as his new job. He had designated himself as my guardian, and from that day on he never wanted me out of his sight. I couldn't be happier.

I was feeling hungry and realized it was already lunchtime. I popped in my favorite Mozart CD. I loved cooking and eating to classical music. And somehow it didn't seem out of place in my rustic log cabin at all. I threw together a spinach and romaine salad with some sweet Vidalia onion and cucumber, added some chunks of ham I had purchased at the deli, and topped it with a pear vinegar and olive oil dressing. I'll need to buy some fresh herbs until I can get the garden in shape. A little dill would have been nice. I talked the whole time I was putting together my lunch; Hoagy seemed to take comfort in the sound of my voice. He truly appeared to be grateful to be here. Amazing. I tossed him a chew treat, it was supposed to be good for his teeth, and then I settled in with my book and a glass of iced tea. Hoagy was making living with a dog very easy.

After lunch I once again hooked Hoagy to his leash. The woman at the shelter said it might take two to three weeks before I could trust him not to try to find his way back to his original home or even to the shelter. I was not willing to risk chasing a runaway dog down the highway. I put on my beautiful red boots and together we went out the door to explore, and in Hoagy's case, sniff and pee. It had turned out to be a perfect spring day. The birds were once again singing loudly and calling to each other through the trees as they tried to find a mate. It was time to make new babies and begin the cycle of life once more. They flitted from tree to tree and branch to branch, in a flurry of activity.

Dried twigs snapped under my feet, and the leaves made a pleasant crunching sound. We walked around the house so Hoagy could learn the smells and sounds of his new place. As we circled back to the front of the house, the river side that is, I stopped for a minute to look down the embankment to the rushing water. In the spring, when the ice and snow is melting, the river moves at a furious pace. Later in the season it will slow down and become that lazy river that we loved to sing about. The water was moving so fast that I had to pull my eyes away from it, because I had a slight feeling of motion sickness. Hoagy would need to be kept away from it at all costs until the slowdown, or he could be swept downstream. Keeping a lab out of the water would be a tough task.

Suddenly his large head turned to the right, he picked up his ears, and cocked his head. I heard it too. Someone was walking through the woods. I was really glad I had a canine companion with me. Soon a figure of a man emerged, and I realized it was Conor. He smiled and waved and Hoagy instantly relaxed. As he got closer and I saw those blue eyes, I once again felt shock waves run through my entire body. I started to step forward, but I stumbled on a tree root that was hidden in the leaves, and almost fell. I have never tripped so much in my life. He must have thought I was a complete klutz. I managed to stay upright and, thereby, save my dignity.

"Hi, beautiful day, isn't it?" He called out. When he got closer, Hoagy went up to him to sniff his hand and all the way around his pant legs. Conor didn't seem to mind a bit. "Hey, who's this fellow? I didn't know you had a dog."

"I just brought him home a few hours ago," I said, trying to still my racing heart. What was going on with me? "I got him at the no-kill shelter. They think he's about 4 years old, so I don't have to worry about a puppy teething on my furniture; plus he was already housebroken." I was babbling and I knew it. It wasn't pretty.

"He's a real beauty. You were lucky. He looks like a purebred English Lab, with that stocky body and broad head. I don't think he would have lasted there too long. Labs are in high demand around here."

"The clerk said he had just been put on the adoption list this morning, and I was the first person through the door. I guess it was meant to be," I said, while stroking his head.

"What's his name?"

"Hoagy."

"Like the sandwich? That's a strange name for a dog."

"Actually, he's named after Hoagy Carmichael."

I expected Conor to say 'who's that?' Instead he looked up at me and said, "Ah, Hoagy, of The Nearness of You and Stardust fame."

"I'm shocked that you know him," I said.

"I play a little piano; he's always been one of my favorites. I especially like the Nora Jones version of The Nearness of You. That's one I don't often own up to, though, especially when the guys are around." Was that a little embarrassment I detected? Interesting. Shock waves, fast beating heart, now Hoagy Carmichael and Nora Jones? Grandpa, are you sending me more messages?

"Well, anyway, I thought it was a nice day for a walk through the path. I wanted to see if there were any downed branches that have to be cleared. I was hoping I would run into you, actually, to see if you had any more work for me. Things have been slow as far as construction goes, and I have free time on my hands right now."

"The only thing I can think of is that I could use a name for a company that can grade my driveway. Do you know of anyone?"

"As it happens, my best friend Jim does that type of thing. He owns large equipment and even works for the City on occasion. I'll get you his number. Do you text?"

"Sure, that would be great." We exchanged cell phone numbers; I felt a strange sense of comfort and security about that.

"Well," he said, as he turned to go, "I have to get back. I need to get Dad to a doctor's appointment."

"Oh, I'm sorry. I never thought to ask how he was doing."

"He's much better now. It's just a follow-up visit. Thanks."

"Okay, then. I'll look for the text. And thanks again for watching the property."

He smiled, and said, "That's what we do around here in Eagle Creek. We take care of each other." And with that he turned and walked back into the trees, with only the sound of his boots crunching the leaves left behind. I immediately felt a sense of loss.

I took a few deep breaths of fresh air before Hoagy and I went back into the house. I was about to become my mother and work myself into a housecleaning frenzy.

I removed my boots at the door and unhooked Hoagy from his leash. He lazily walked toward his bone, and laid down with a thump for a good chew, but I noticed how he positioned his body so his eyes could follow me around the house. He seemed to be grateful for the chance at having a new home; it was as if he didn't want to lose me in case he had to go back. I've never known such a relaxed and laid back dog. He was perfect for me, and my heart swelled with love. We were already completely bonded. Too bad human relationships didn't work this easily. I poured a cup of coffee, but I noticed it was cold. The coffee maker had automatically turned off, so I popped the mug into the microwave. In a few seconds it was deliciously warm again. Oh, it was so good. I wondered when I would be able to buy something this rich and mellow again. Maybe on the Internet. I flipped open my laptop that I had left on the countertop since I first arrived. Funny that it had never occurred to me to check my email. I guess I was starting to unplug from city life. Just as I suspected, there is no area-wide WiFi out here. I'm going to have to call someone about getting an Internet provider, I thought. Another thing for the to-do list.

I spent hours doing the routine housecleaning jobs; dusting, vacuuming, cleaning bathrooms, and washing the few windows that I could reach. I even cleaned the refrigerator and stove, inside and out.

Just as I finished and was admiring my work, my cell phone buzzed. I grabbed it and saw a text from Conor with his friend's phone number and the message, "Do U need anything else?"

"Who do I call 4 Internet service?"

"Riverside Cable."

"Thx"

Our communication was short and to the point. We had only known each other for two days and with very little chance to get to know each other, at that. Did I want more? It's possible, but I planned to tread lightly. I had a broken heart that needed repair, and even though it had been several years, old wounds were recently opened.

Now, back to work, I told myself. The house was clean and presentable, and I felt very comfortable showing it to anyone else who may come to visit. So it's on to the next task of going through my parents' closets and drawers. It just didn't seem right somehow. It was almost like snooping when I was a kid, but this time there was no chance of getting caught. I headed up the stairs with Hoagy at my heels.

The main room of the loft had a pullout bed which is where I had been sleeping. I loved looking out at the river and watching for wildlife. I wasn't ready to sleep in my parents' room yet; one of these days, when this really feels like my house, I'll probably take the room on the north side. That room has a large window which looks toward the wooded path that leads to Conor's house. Of course, that is not the reason I'd want that room. At least that is what I was telling myself.

After a few hours of sorting through clothes, I stopped a moment to stretch and rub my back. Reaching, bending, and standing again had finally taken its toll. I sat on the edge of the bed and looked around at the beautiful room. My mother had always loved beautiful things. She had kept several pieces that had belonged to my grandparents and added a few of her own, making a sort of mishmash of styles and eras, but it all seemed to work. The pressed back oak rocker in the corner was her favorite place to sit and work on piecing quilt blocks. Grandma had taught her at a young age to use a needle and thread, and my mother had done the same for me. Lily was never interested in sewing or anything to do with the past. She preferred to "live in the moment" as she used to say, and never understood my passion for the art of quilting. I've always felt a great sense of pleasure when I hold cotton in my hands, carefully fitting triangles and squares together to make a pattern. I was hoping to find time to quilt again, real soon. The room on the opposite side of the loft room would be my sewing area. I have so many plans, but if I didn't keep moving along, here, I'll never get them all done.

As my eyes scanned the room, I noticed the

boxes on the top shelf of the closet. Luckily, I had carried a small stepstool upstairs just in case. I was used to the fact that my short stature required a boost now and then to reach high places. I raised myself up on my toes and reached for the round hatbox decorated in a delicate rose pattern. Although reminiscent of an age gone by, it was actually smaller than a normal hat box, and it looked to be a reproduction. I had thought this was one of the many boxes that held old family photos, but now I saw that it seemed to have another purpose. I carefully stepped down from the stool, and sat the box on the bed. On the top was written "Kate" in black Magic Marker. I picked up the box again and shook it, an old habit of mine. I always shook packages before opening them, and many times the gift giver would say, "Stop, you'll break your present." This time all I heard was a thump as the item moved around the box. I carefully lifted the lid and discovered a soft leather book, a journal of some sort. I flipped opened the pages and saw my grandmother's perfect handwriting, from an era when the correct slant and graceful cursive letters were highly regarded. But why was there a book that was just meant for me? And how did she know I would find it here? When had she written it? She'd been gone for many years. My curiosity overtook my normal sense of completing one job before beginning something else. Besides, as I looked around me, I realized I was pretty much finished anyway. I had sorted the clothes into piles to throw out and placed some in bags to take to Goodwill. My back was not up to carrying these heavy bags down the stairs right now. Maybe tomorrow.

"Come, Hoagy." He opened his eyes from his slumber on the rug, raised one eyebrow, and without complaint got up and followed me down the steps. It was time for his supper and mine, too, and then I would settle in and begin reading Grandma Sophie's journal, and find out what message she had left for me so many years after her death.

⌘ Chapter Six ⌘

Kate - 2014

Hoagy and I were both quite hungry. A glance at the clock told me it was way past the hour I had planned to feed him in order to stay on the same feeding schedule the shelter had been on. I picked up his new bowl, and ordered him to sit and stay. I am always surprised when he obeys. I'm sure he's been to obedience school, and knows a lot more commands than I am aware of. I filled his bowl, placed it on the floor, and said "okay." Watching him dive in was a treat. What joy dogs take from the simple pleasure of food, and it doesn't even matter if he eats the same thing day after day.

Since I am not of the canine persuasion, though, I like quite a variety in my diet. I grabbed a large pot and filled it with water, threw in some salt that I measured out in the palm of my hand, just as my grandmother had taught me, and while I was waiting for it to boil, I grabbed some basil I had in a glass of water in the fridge. I dropped a few handfuls in the food processor along with some pine nuts and garlic, and then I streamed in some extra virgin olive oil. The smell of the basil permeated the room. Next, I added the Parmesan cheese. My basil pesto was ready for the pasta. The water had begun to boil so I dropped in enough pasta for two people; I always make more than I need so I can have the leftovers for another meal. There, in ten minutes, I'll have a very nice meal for one. Simple but good. I wished I had thought to bring a nice loaf of French bread so I could make my own garlic bread. I put that on the list I had already started for my next trip to the store. But for now, I was very satisfied with my pesto pasta, and I decided to try some Chardonnay from Leelanau Cellars; it's not like me to open a bottle of wine when another one is already open, but I had picked up a few different bottles on my way here yesterday. Michigan is becoming very well known for its wines, and I wanted to be a true Michigander once again. Was it only yesterday that I first arrived? I was feeling very good about what I had accomplished so far.

"Hoagy, what should we listen to today while enjoying our simple Italian meal?" Already in a doggie snooze after filling his belly, he lifted his head at the sound of his name, and raised an eyebrow. "How about Andrea Bocelli? That should set the tone for our dining experience quite nicely. Besides he's one of my favorites and you should get to know him."

He sighed and lowered his head to his paws, but his eyes remained on me, almost as if he was trying to figure out what I was talking about. I slipped in the CD, and the first song on the album filled the air. Besame Mucho. Well, so much for Italian music. This 1940s Bolero, was actually written by a Mexican, and then re-recorded by the Beatles with a different beat. But somehow even when Andrea Bocelli sings in Spanish, it still sounds Italian, so I'm good. I never cared to eat alone, but just the same, my meal was very satisfying. I decided to leave the dishes until later, hoping Mom wasn't looking down at this big no-no. I was anxious to start reading.

I carried the journal and glass of wine to the

couch, and of course, Hoagy, got up to follow me, lowered himself on the beautiful Native American style area rug at my feet. Now that we were both settled, I could get started on reading whatever it was my grandmother had left for me. I opened the supple leather cover slowly. It felt good in my hands, knowing that my beloved grandmother had held it also. Just touching it flooded me with memories of kisses and cookies. A folded letter, which had been tucked in the pages of the journal, fluttered to the floor. The papers were old and brittle; it was obvious they had been creased for a long time.

October 15, 1994

Dear Sweet Kate,

From the time you were a child you were always so inquisitive. 'What's this, Grandma? Why do daffodils only bloom in the spring? Why do rabbits always eat your crocuses? How do you know how to make a quilt? Why do you always put salt in the macaroni water?' Why, Why, Why. Sometimes I admit to being tired of answering your questions, but as you grew to become a beautiful young woman, I knew that your curiosity would serve you well. It was always strange to me that your sister, Lily, has none of that curiosity at all. You two are so different for being twins. She was, and is still, so logical. Everything for her is black and white with no room for gray. She wants what she wants and when she wants it, while you have always had a romantic idea of the past, and were willing to wait for things to happen. You liked to slowly and carefully delve into a subject, deeply seeking out the answers you were looking for. I was not at all surprised you became a librarian and went into family research as a specialty. I think it all started that year in school when you had to do a project which required you to create a family tree. Suddenly, you wanted to know who you were and where you came from. Remember how I helped you as we filled in the names and dates on your family chart? As soon as you became aware of your ancestry, you wanted to know everything about your German great-grandparents and then later your paternal Polish grandparents.

You were so young then, and I didn't feel the time was right to tell you the whole story, so I decided to wait until you asked again, and then take it one step at a time. As you continued your search throughout the years, your genealogy quest was so far back in time that you never asked about your great-grandparents again. I heard you talk about branches that were taking you back to Charlemagne in the 700s and other exciting lines that tie in to royalty. This year you turned twenty, and I decided the best thing to do was tell my story and leave it for you. If you ask me about the past again before I part this earth, I will gladly tell you everything I know then; otherwise, I leave my journal for you to inherit. I know you are the one who will truly appreciate this story and maybe look into it further. I want you to know that I hold no hard feelings against anyone, but only feel sadness for what could have been. Feel free to dig deeply. I encourage you to do so, as a matter of fact. By the time you will be reading this, we will all be long gone, and there should be no one left behind to get hurt.

> *You're loving and adoring grandmother,*
> *Sophia Wilhelmina Bauer Klein*

I lowered the letter to my lap, slightly dazed.

What in the world was my grandmother about to tell me that she felt she had to hide away for so long? My mother must have known about this also, or else how could this journal have been in the hatbox on her top shelf, yet Mother never once gave a hint of this family mystery. My hands were shaking with anticipation as I began to turn to the first written page. This is just the sort of thing that I loved to solve for others as they came to my desk in the family history room at the library. But this time, it was my family's story and the feelings of what I might discover were quite a bit different.

Suddenly, my cell phone rang, startling me. I had been living without Internet and TV for the past few days, and the sound of the outside world intruding was almost upsetting. I reached for the phone and glanced at the caller ID – Cara. It was just like her to read my thoughts and feel the need to call. "Hi, Miss Worm," I said using our old nickname for each other, referring to the bookworms that we both were.

"Hey, Worm," she said. "How are things in

the woods?"

"It's wonderful. I'm feeling so relaxed. I'm really settling in. And big news – I have a dog," I told her, excitedly.

"A dog? That's wonderful. I know how you have always loved dogs and wanted one for your own, but you-know-who was allergic."

"Yeah, well my life is my own, on all counts now, so getting Hoagy was one of the first things I wanted to do here."

"Hoagy?" she asked. "Where did that name come from?"

"Believe it or not it was the name he came with, so I decided to keep it since, for me, it refers to Hoagy Carmichael. I think it was just meant to be."

"Oh yeah, your family's fixation on old music. What breed is he?"

"He's a beautiful yellow lab, but in the most pure white color. He's watching me as we speak, trying to figure out what kind of psychic/mindreader I'm talking to," I said jokingly.

"What do you mean?"

"Cara, the librarian in you is going to love this. My grandmother left me a letter and a journal," I said. "Apparently, there's more to my family history than I knew. The journal supposedly has some insight into a secret, and, in her letter, she is asking me to continue looking into it."

"Wow, I wish I could be there to help." I could hear the wheels turning as she went into research mode. "Is there anything I can do from this end? Do you have Internet service yet?"

"No," I said. "I was planning to call first thing in the morning. I hope it doesn't take too long to hook me up to cable."

"Well, what do you know so far? Fill me in."

"I was just beginning to read the first page of the journal when you called. I'm really stumped as to what this could mean; I thought I had all of the facts about my family already. I'll call first thing tomorrow after I've had time to read further. Thanks for the offer of help. I appreciate it."

"Anything for you, Miss Worm, you know that," she said. "So tell me. Have you met any good-looking rednecks yet?"

I laughed. Always the matchmaker, Cara couldn't help but think of making everyone around her happy. "As a matter of fact," I said quietly, "there is someone I might be interested in." I heard a girly squeal from the other end, and so did Hoagy. "Now don't get all excited -- I said, might! But he has the most gorgeous blue eyes and there is something so familiar about him. Oh, and get this, he actually knows who Hoagy Carmichael is!"

"Sounds like a match made in Heaven right there. Did you check the ring finger? If it's empty, let me know when the wedding is. Just pick a good color for the maid of honor dress. You know how fussy I am about tints and hues!"

"Cara, please, I've only had two conversations with him, and it was short at that." I blushed at the memory of the first time he "saw" me. Good thing she couldn't see through the phone; Cara would have picked up on that right away.

"I've really got to go. I'm anxious to read my grandma's journal."

"Okay, email me as soon as your Internet service is running. Then we can Skype. I'll talk to you again in a few days. Bye bye, Worm."

Okay, back to the book. I put my phone on vibrate and placed it on the table near me. Buzz, buzz. Now what? Cara must be calling back with something she had forgotten to say. But a quick look at the phone showed that it was Conor. I wondered what he could want. I hesitated a second, gathered my thoughts, took a deep breath, and then answered.

"Hello?" I said, trying to sound as if I didn't know who it was.

"Hi, Kate. This is Conor." His voice was like fog and honey at the same time; just a little fuzzy, but smooth and oh so pleasant to listen to. "I hope I'm not interrupting anything."

"No, no. Not at all," I said. "I'm just reading and relaxing after a long day."

"Well, I was just, ah, thinking," he said, sounding a little unsure of himself, "would you be interested in grabbing a cup of coffee with me in the morning? I mean, more like mid- morning; I like to take a break about 10:00 at Brewster's. It's right on the main drag near the dam. You can't miss it."

"Oh, I guess I could. Sure, why not? I need to get out and check out the town."

"Okay, great! I'll be at the table near the back door. It's my regular spot."

"All right. I'll see you there." Well, I was hoping for another encounter with Mr. Conor McAuley, although I had not expected it to happen quite so soon, but that was just fine with me. I took a deep breath and smiled to myself, because I had something quite pleasant to look forward to in the morning. Now, I needed to focus and get back to the journal.

I began to read my grandmother's clear and beautiful script.

⌘ Chapter Seven ⌘

Sophie – 1944

I absolutely worshiped my big sister, Hattie. She was sixteen, eight years older than me, and she was able to wear lipstick and heels. I loved watching her get ready for a night out with her friends. I sat next to her as she carefully applied her powder and rouge, and fluffed and patted her hair, making sure that each Victory roll and wave was perfectly in place. I was the privileged one who got to decide if the lines she drew down the back of her tanned legs were straight, imitating a nylon seam. Tanning legs had become a necessity for a perfectly groomed young woman. At the start of World War II, the government had banned the import of silk from Japan, and now even nylon was required for the war effort in making parachutes. Faking the look of wearing nylons had inspired girls to get creative.

"Hattie, why do you call your hairdo 'Victory

Rolls' "? I asked with my chin in my hands.

"Well, sweetie, it's supposed to look like an airplane rolling a victory dance in the air after shooting down a German or a Jap," she explained patiently. "It's just one of the many things we can do to encourage our boys in the war."

"What else do you do, Hattie?"

"We hold Victory dances at the Armory, and when our boys come home on leave, before going overseas, we dance the night away, and show them a good time. We're lucky to have the Armory for the entire River County right here in our town. Mama says it's a wonderful way to help the boys' disposition and prepare them for war. It only costs 10 cents to get in, but every penny they raise can help in some small way."

"I wish I was older so I could go with you," I said wistfully.

"Me too, squirt. But your time will come soon enough. I only hope for your sake that the war is over by then. So, how do I look?" she asked as she twisted around trying to see the rear view of herself *in the mirror.*

"You look beautiful," I said with a jealous sigh. When will my turn come to wear jewelry and make-up, I wondered?

She smoothed her hands over her hips and straightened her collar, did a little twirl, and said, "Come on, help me practice my dance steps." Hattie grabbed my hands and we began to hum 'In the Mood' as we danced the Jitterbug just the way she had taught me. We collapsed on the bed in giggles. It must be so much fun to be sixteen!

My next memory is several months later; summer was in full swing, and the pinching June bugs were beating at the screens at night while I tried to sleep. They always scared me, but as long as I was indoors when it was dark, I felt a little safer. Recent news of the Normandy Invasion had reached us. Everyone was very concerned about their sons, brothers, boyfriends, and husbands. We had heard there was a terrible loss of lives, and even though the adults tried to hide things from the children, we still knew they were all worried that

one of those horrible telegrams would arrive
announcing the death of a loved one. Soon after
that awful knock on the door, the blue star in the
window, given out by The Blue Star Mothers to any
mother who had a son in the war, would be replaced
with a gold star, for the one who had lost his life.

I remember Hattie was not herself then. She
wrote letters to the boy who lived through the
woods, named Ryan McAuley. Our parents knew
the McAuleys well, and Hattie had always had a
crush on Ryan, even though he was at least four
years older. She told me they used to dance together
and had a lot of laughs. But now, she cried a lot and
stayed in her room most afternoons, saying she was
hot and wanted to sit by the fan, but I knew
something else was wrong. I think she had fallen in
love. If this was love, it sure seemed miserable to
me. I'm not so sure I wanted anything to do with it.

One day, I was trying to find Ration, my cat.
She was from a litter belonging to one of our
neighbor's cats who kept having babies at regular
intervals. She was named Ration when Mama said,

if only they would ration cats instead of food we would be a lot better off. I loved Ration, but she had a way of getting herself into trouble. She loved sneaking around in the woods, and surprising the birds. I hated it when she brought home a mangled mess of feathers and presented it at my feet. One of her favorite hiding spots was under the porch. There was an opening at one end so I crawled in and inched on my belly behind the cross-hatching. There she was. She came to me, rubbed her head against my leg and purred. I was about to back out with her, when I realized that Mama and Hattie were above me on the porch swing. Hattie was crying and Mama was speaking softly, in a comforting tone. There was nothing I loved more in this world than listening in on adult conversations. Most of the time it made no sense; some of the words were new to me. How did they learn all of those big words, anyway? I stayed right where I was and quietly tried to figure out what was going on.

"Mama, how can I go on without knowing?" Hattie sobbed.

"Don't worry, honey. It will be all right," said Mama.

"Should I tell the McAuleys what he means to me? Will it hurt them to know, or will it be a help for them to know that he was loved?"

"Well," said Mama, "I'm sure they'll be surprised, that's for sure, but it might bring them some comfort. We had no idea you two were so close. I mean, I knew you had a few dances and you were writing to him at basic training, but I thought the letters were just because you were volunteering for the war effort. We still think of you as children running and playing in the woods. I don't think any of us knew you were a couple. Here, take my hankie."

"Thank you," Hattie said blowing her nose. "We wanted to keep it a secret, because I am still only 16 and he is 20. We thought we would tell everyone when he came home. But now, what does this mean for us? MIA – I might never see him again." And with that she burst out in uncontrollable sobs.

MIA. What does that mean? That was a new one to me. I'd have to see if I could figure it out without giving away my listening spot.

"Come, honey. Let's go inside. I'll get you some tea and you can try to get some rest," said Mama.

I heard the porch floorboards creak and then the screen door bang. Mama must be very distracted, because we were never allowed to bang the door.

I soon learned about MIA – Missing in Action. Some of the soldiers would never be heard from again, while others would be found later with units other than their own after having been separated from their company. At the end of the war, some of the missing would be discovered in POW camps. Now, for Hattie and the McAuleys, it would be a waiting game. Each day more difficult than the last.

I supposed some time had passed, but I am not quite sure how much. I was still a child, after all, chasing butterflies, and picking wildflowers to

bring home to my mother. She loved my flowers
and always put them in a vase on the table. It made
me feel special. I was in a world of my own,
enjoying each summer day from morning to dusk. I
didn't pay too much attention to my sister, except
that she was quiet and moody. I guess, she was just
plain sad, and I didn't really know how to deal with
it, so I didn't.

A few weeks, or maybe months, later, I was
once again in a position to listen in on a talk that
was not meant for my ears. I took full advantage of
the situation. The sheets were hanging on the line to
dry, and a breeze was blowing, moving them in
gentle waves. I loved running between them as the
wet fabric slapped at me. I had been told many
times not to play in the sheets as they were drying,
but it was so refreshing on this hot day, that I
couldn't resist.

Mama and Hattie were walking out with a
laundry basket ready to hang more clothes. I stood
very still, trying to figure out how I could escape
without being caught playing in my white flapping

tent.

I heard Mama say, "I talked to Papa about it, last night."

"Oh, no! You didn't," exclaimed Hattie.

"Well, child, I had no choice. We have to figure this out, and I needed some help," said Mama with a sigh. "Here, sit in the shade with me." Amazingly, they did not seem to notice my scuffed, brown leather, Mary Janes sticking out under the sheets, totally exposing my feet.

"We have no choice, now," I heard Mama say. "Something has to be done soon. We have no idea when, or if, Ryan will come home. I know that hurts, honey, but it's true."

"I hate this stupid war," said Hattie. "It's ruined everything. I know I should feel more patriotic, but I just want my life to be normal, again."

"Well, it isn't the same as it used to be, and it never will be again," said Mama patiently. "Now, it's time to grow up so you can deal with this situation. You're still young and you have your *whole life ahead of you."*

"So, what do I do?" asked Hattie.

"Papa and I have arranged for you to go visit Aunt Lucy in Traverse City. She's been having a hard time lately. She has some arthritis problems and with no children of her own, she has no one to help out with the housework."

"Oh, Mama, that's so far away," cried Hattie, "and I don't have any friends there."

"Lucy will introduce you to new people, and when she is feeling better and you are up to it, you can come back home. It will only be for a few months. Time will fly by, you'll see."

"I guess if I must, but I won't like it." I could imagine Hattie pouting, in that teenage girl way.

I worked my way down to the end of the sheets, and took off running toward the wood pile before anyone noticed I had been there the whole time. I knew I wouldn't like it while Hattie was gone, but I guess Aunt Lucy needed her. I hoped when I grew up Mama didn't send me off to a relative. You can take family charity too far in my opinion!

Hattie left a few weeks later. She sent me regular letters and it seemed as if her spirits were lifting. She had made some friends and seemed to enjoy living in cherry country. Later in the year, I think it was after Thanksgiving, Mama said she was worried about her sister and she missed Hattie. She wanted to go see them for herself. She told me she was leaving on the train in the morning, and Papa and I would be home alone. Mrs. McAuley would take care of me after school, while Papa worked. She promised she wouldn't be gone long and assured me she would be home for Christmas. She even hinted at having a very special present for me this year.

The next morning Papa and I took her to the train station and when I hugged her tight, I noticed she was a little bit rounder than she had been before. I wanted to be brave, so I did not cry, but I was terrified she would go MIA, also. The weeks passed.

Mrs. McAuley usually had cookies and milk for me after school; I did my homework while listening to their radio. On Saturdays she let me listen to Little Orphan Annie, Cisco Kid, and The Green Hornet, and soon I was told that Mama and Hattie were coming home. I was so excited.

One afternoon, Papa and I got all dressed up and he drove us to the train station. I was so anxious to see them both that I could hardly sit still, but a piece of licorice and my new yo-yo kept me busy. Soon the train was pulling into the station and Mama and Hattie were getting off. Papa rushed to help with the bags and give them both a kiss. Hattie bent down, picked me right off the ground, and twirled me around. It looked like Mama had some laundry or something in her hands. She carefully squatted down to my level and showed me the bundle.

"Sophie, look what I have for you," she said

But what kind of present was that? It was a baby!

"A baby? I didn't ask for a baby! Where did it come from?"

Mama then explained that his name was

James but we'll call him Jamie. He is my new brother, and he was born while Mama was visiting Aunt Lucy. Now until that time, I had been perfectly happy being the baby in the family. I was not so sure I was going to like this new addition which would push me out of my coveted position. I was now going to be a middle child! I have to admit to not being very pleasant to live with for a few weeks, but I soon adjusted to the new person in my life, and I was so happy to have Hattie and Mama back that I forgave them both quickly.

When Jamie was born I was eight years old. Because of the age difference, we didn't have a lot in common, but I learned how to take care of a baby by watching and helping Mama. Hattie went on with her life. The McAuleys had not heard a thing about Ryan. He had been missing for almost a year. Hattie got a job in the local dimestore selling records, and there she met a young man who had not been accepted into the armed forces, because of his flat feet. He was a record salesman, and since she saw him once a week, they got to know each other quickly. They flirted and teased and he took her out to dinner on occasion. They shared a love of music and dancing, and listening to the latest Glenn Miller and Tommy Dorsey songs. Girls were getting married very young then; it was common for a girl to wed at 17 and 18, and Hattie did the same. Her husband got a new job in St Joseph, so they moved in order to begin their life there. It was a good thing that she moved away, because Ryan had been discovered in a POW camp and returned home in 1945 as soon as the war was over. I'll never know how he felt about finding that Hattie had married; maybe he was not in love with her as much as she was with him. She might have been just a last fling before going off to war. It was never discussed in front of me, and eventually Ryan, too, found someone to love and married a girl named Roma. After such a long absence, and his horrible experience during the war, he decided to stay right here in River County near his family, where he could find comfort and security with those who loved him.

By 1953, at the age of 17, I had met Carl. We

had the same German Lutheran background, and sense of humor; we were a perfect match. By 1954 I was married, and soon after, I was pregnant with our first child, who would become your mother, Mary.

Now, Kate, here is the part that I have been building up to. Throughout these years the McAuley family had remained close with ours. There were picnics and parties on the river bank, and lots of backyard cookouts by an open fire. Ryan and Roma had three lovely children, one a girl named Cindy. She was just a few years younger than Jamie. When Jamie was 15, he suddenly began to look at Cindy in a new light. She was beautiful, with her fair Irish coloring, red hair, and green eyes. She attracted a lot of attention from the local boys, but she seemed to have eyes only for Jamie. I believe it went no further than hand-holding, because this was a different time than today. Courtship moved a lot slower, but that was also the reason for young marriages. When it became clear that you could no longer control your hormones, you got married.

At some point, mother became aware that Jamie and Cindy were flirting and knew they might want to start dating. That meant she had to face something she had been putting off for far too long. She knew the time was right for her to have a talk with Jamie, but not the one he would expect. This talk was about the birds and bees, all right, but also would be much more upsetting for him. She now had to reveal her secret, one that only Papa, Mama, Aunt Lucy, and Hattie knew, and one that I had long suspected, having gone over and over memories from when I was younger. Mama was not Jamie's mother – Hattie was. Now, the McAuleys had no knowledge of this at all. Mama had managed to keep the secret even from her best friend. But now, Mama was forced to tell Jamie because she could not let this infatuation with Cindy continue. She would have to inform Jamie of something he would not want to hear – that Cindy was his half sister.

Of course, Jamie was devastated and he was embarrassed, but most of all he was hurt. He had just lost his girlfriend, his mother, and father in one blow. And then there was the confusion of why Hattie, his real mother, didn't want him, or why had she not owned up to it after she got married. He was still a baby when she got married; she could have taken him with her and he would have never known the difference. Instead, she had gone on to raise a family in another city and rarely even visited. His nieces and nephews, he now realized, were actually his siblings. Maybe Hattie was afraid of tipping her hand, or maybe she had never even told her husband, and was afraid of losing him. Mama told Jamie that he could never tell Cindy why but he could no longer see her as a girlfriend. Her father, Ryan, had no knowledge of this deceit. All relationships between the families would be severed forever, so he was banned from approaching his biological father.

There was some slamming of doors, with Jamie throwing things around in his room. Papa tried to talk him out of his fury, but finally they both decided to leave him alone to work it out for himself. In the morning, Mama was hoping he might have *calmed down a bit. She made his favorite breakfast of blueberry pancakes and bacon. He was usually down by seven o'clock at the latest, but today there was no sound of movement from the upstairs bedroom. She climbed the stairs and tiptoed into his room and quietly peeked in, but his room was empty. The bed was unmade and probably had not been slept in all night. Jamie was gone. There was a short note on his pillow that said: I don't know where I am going. Don't try to find me. You will never see me again.*

And this, my dear Kate, is where my story ends. We never did hear from Jamie, again. Papa and Mama wrote letters and made calls to relatives in other cities, but there was no sign of him. The pain was so great for my parents that after a while, they did not even mention his name. Hattie on the other hand was not very concerned, or so it seemed. After all, she had never developed any kind of bond with Jamie, and after years of denying him as a son, I think she started to believe it herself. I realize now, what a selfish streak Hattie had, or maybe it was just the times we were living in, when having a child out of wedlock was a shame to a family and had to be hidden away. Once Mama offered a solution, she wiped the problem from her mind completely. But one never knows what is truly in a person's thoughts. Maybe the torture of giving up her son was just too much for her and the only way to cope was to block out his existence in order to ensure her own survival.

So now you see, that your family tree is not accurate at all. Your great-uncle Jamie did not die as a young man, as we told you when you first began doing genealogy; he simply ran away. Perhaps something awful did happen to him and we were never told, or maybe he found his place in the world and went on to live a productive life. Either way, if you want an accurate picture on your charts, you have some adjusting to do. And maybe there is still a trail to be followed. The rest is up to you. At this point it doesn't really matter who knows Mama's big secret. So I leave this story in your hands.

Your loving grandmother,
Sophie Klein

⌘ Chapter Eight ⌘

Kate – 2014

I stared at the pages in shock and confusion. My mind was spinning with the distorted family connections and how it related to me. I had read slowly and carefully, making notes as I went along, but I would need a second or even third reading to be clear on facts and dates. I wanted to go into detective mode right now, doing what I do best. I loved nothing more than sorting out these family lines, but I was truly exhausted. I needed to save this information for morning when I would have a clear head. It was not a close enough connection to me to have an emotional effect; I had never known Jamie, and only met Great-Aunt Hattie a few times before her death. But still it was part of my heritage, and I wanted to find out the rest of the story. What happened to Jamie? Is he still living? And if so, where? Does he have a family? Grandma had given me so much to think about, but not now. My eyes were heavy, and a soft bed was calling. First though, I needed to take Hoagy out for a short walk before bedtime. I grabbed the flashlight by the door and hooked on his leash. I didn't plan to go far since it was starting to get dark already. Tomorrow I planned to explore the woods and stroll through my property. But tonight, a quick walk to the river bank would have to be enough.

It was a beautiful evening, still and serene. The sun was just going down over the river casting a variety of shadows on the water. There were two fishermen in a small motorboat downriver packing up their things and getting ready to call it a night. Some last minute birds were flocking and taking shelter in the trees, calling out raucously to each as if they were going to a late-night party. I spotted a doe on the opposite bank, quietly grazing on some new grasses and buds. She raised her eyes and stared at me with a steady gaze, all the while, switching her white flag tail. I knew that was a signal of possible danger; there must be others nearby she was motioning to. Maybe her twins were hiding in the bushes, trusting their mother to watch over them. When she was sure I was not a threat, she continued her meal – a munch here, a bite there.

Hoagy was sniffing around looking for just the right spot, so I stood there in the stillness, and contemplated some of the new facts I had just learned. I wish I had someone to talk to about it. When I get inside I'll call Cara, of course, but there was a time when I had a husband to come home to and tell all about the day's events. I used to talk to my sister every day, but she had rarely been interested in anything I had to say. She was usually distracted by her job, or someone or something else. She never seemed to have time or interest in me. It took me years, and one very major event, to finally realize, that even though we were twins, we would never be like some twins are, reading each others' minds and finishing each others' sentences. I finally gave up, knowing it was a waste of time to keep trying. And later I didn't want to ever hear from her again; the hurt was too great, and I needed to separate myself from her for my own preservation.

So I made a conscious effort to wipe her from my mind.

A small whinny nearby startled me out of my reverie. It was a screech owl, a strange name for a bird that actually sounds like a horse. I couldn't see it, but it must be right above my head. Hoagy was done with his business, so now that I was assured of not having to get up in the middle of the night with him, I turned and walked slowly towards the comforting glow showing through the bamboo blinds of my log lodge. Tomorrow I would see Conor for coffee. I'll have to decide then if I'm ready to share what I know about the McAuley family's part in my family history.

Morning came way too soon, it was 7:00 already, but I felt rested and ready to start the day. Sleep has always been just a necessity for me; there always seems to be so much to do and so little time. I never understood how people could sleep all weekend and talk about "catching up," staying in bed until noon. But here in River County, life had slowed down considerably, and I was actually able to enjoy sleeping. I was no longer waking up with clenched fists or a clamped jaw. My whole body was relaxed, fresh, and eager to see what was in store for me today. Hoagy heard me moving around. He jumped up from his guard position on the rug at the side of my bed, and gave a little bark. It was obvious that he too had stuff to do - another trip outside and then it would be time to get his breakfast.

"Okay, boy, give me a minute to get my bearings," I said with a yawn.

He cocked his head and whimpered back at me. "Well, I guess I can have a two-way conversation with you." I jumped out of bed and pulled a sweatshirt over my tee. I made sure to zip it up this time. I wasn't planning on running into anybody, but I hadn't been yesterday, either. I did not plan to make that mistake again!

After Hoagy's quick trip outside, I lowered his bowl to the floor and watched as he eagerly lapped up every bite and continued to lick until any trace of flavor was erased.

I made myself some decaf herbal tea and a

piece of toast. I decided to eat light, since I might want something with my coffee later. When I was finished, I called the cable service, and discovered that even though there is service available, the cable runs down the main road. Since I am a quarter of a mile off that road, I would have to pay by the foot for the cable to be run through the trees, at a dollar a foot. I grabbed my phone calculator and punched in the numbers – 5280 feet in a mile, divided by 4 for my quarter-mile, equals 1380 feet! Therefore $1380, too rich for my budget at the moment. No Internet? I hadn't even thought that would be a possibility. I always thought the reason Mom and Dad didn't have it at the lodge was because they weren't interested. I was so disappointed. I guess, after coffee my next stop would be the library. I needed to check out their available computers; I hoped I could have access to a genealogy service if I needed it. I had wanted to stop in anyway, so this latest development gave me a good excuse.

After my tea and toast, I climbed the stairs and headed to my mother's room again; I carried all the bags down that I wanted to donate to Goodwill. I thought I would take them into town with me; it was best this far out of town to plan errand runs in order to save gas and time. I'll drop some of the other bags in the large trash container at the end of the driveway. It's was left there for easy access for the garbage trucks.

One more trip up the stairs to change my top and run a brush through my hair. With the loft steps, and walking Hoagy, there will be no need for trips to the gym, that's for sure. Now, what should I do about Hoagy? He hadn't been with me long enough yet to leave him alone. Since it was a perfect day for a Michigan spring and it was a comfortable temperature of 65 degrees with no humidity, I decided it would be okay for him to ride along and wait for me in the car. I think he'd feel more secure with that idea than being left behind. I grabbed a bottle of water and a small bowl from the cupboard just in case he got thirsty, and threw a few treats in my pocket. Owning a dog was turning out to be just like having a new baby in the house, without the crying and sleepless nights. I was not used to taking care of someone other than myself, and having to anticipate their every need, but it felt good nevertheless. When I called him to the car, he seemed thrilled with the prospect of another outing. He hopped right in the passenger seat, but I had heard it was best, safety-wise, for dogs to be in the back, the same as for children, so even though I would have loved having him on the seat beside me, I did the responsible thing and moved him to the back seat. He was okay with that also, standing up and immediately getting a wet smear on my window as he looked out to see where we were going. I realized I'd better get used to having a dirty window; I think it would be like that a lot. I cranked the window down just enough for him to get some air but not enough to let his head stick out the window. I drove down my grooved road, bouncing along in every rut. I sure hoped it would be graded today as promised. I turned left onto the highway, toward the village of Eagle Creek. The road was gently rolling, first down into the thick trees and then back up for a fantastic view of first the river and then the clearings which were used as farmland, going acres back to the next tree line. Everything was so green, it was almost blinding. After living in the city for so long, I had forgotten what a high it is in the spring when color comes flooding back to nature.

As I came to the village, my heart started to pound. I would be walking into a café where I knew no one but Conor. I was not used to doing things on my own; I had always had first my sister, then a husband or my best friend with me. I hoped Conor would be there already waiting at the back table where he had said he would be. The village was only two blocks long, so it wasn't difficult to find Brewster's. There was ample parking in front, but that would mean parallel parking which I wasn't too good at. I quickly spotted a sign and arrow – Parking in the Rear. Relief, no need to embarrass myself, then, with my incompetent skills. I turned down a small alleyway and came out to a large parking lot running the whole length of the block. After a few comforting words to Hoagy, I walked through the back door of Brewster's, and just as he said, he was there at the first table by the door.

Conor's face lit up with a big smile, almost as if he had not been sure I would show up. "Hi," he said jumping up from his chair. "I'm glad you came."

"It was nice of you to invite me," I replied. "I really wanted to check out your local coffee shop, but I'm not much for doing things by myself." He started to pull out my chair and then realized that it might be a little formal, and besides the chairs were quite close to each other, not allowing for much chivalry, so he awkwardly sat back down.

"What kind of coffee can I get here?" I asked.

"Anything you like, from, lattes to mochas, skim, low-fat, decaf, and organic. The menu is on the chalkboard on the wall." He pointed behind the counter. "And the baked goods are fantastic! I meet the guys here every day for a short break. It makes it difficult to keep my figure," he joked.

He pointed to a table at the other end. Four guys in construction-type garb, suddenly lowered their heads, pretending they had not been looking at me. One tried to hide a little smirk, while another jabbed at him, signaling he should act cool.

"I'm sorry to break your routine," I said. "Why did you invite me? Is there something special you want to talk about?"

"No, I thought you might like to meet a few people."

"That was very thoughtful of you. I'm not really shy, but I don't like new situations and walking into large groups of people by myself. It's always been a thing with me."

"Why is that, do you suppose?"

"I'm a twin, so there has always been another person with me, since before I was born."

He raised an eyebrow in surprise. "Are you identical twins?"

"No, but we look enough alike to confuse some people. My parents never confused us, neither did any of my other relatives; once you get to know us, you could easily tell us apart. We could never fool teachers and friends after we had been around them for a while, but our profile, the back of our heads, and certain mannerisms have caused some mistaken identities on more than one occasion."

"Really," he said thoughtfully. "Are you close to your sister?"

I lowered my eyes and hesitated before answering. Just how much did I want him to know? "No, not at all," I said making an instant decision that I could trust this man not to make judgments or spread gossip. "We never were as close as some twins are, and a few years ago we had a falling out. Then recently there was another incident that caused a wedge between us that will remain forever."

"It sounds like you've been hurt. What about forgiveness?" he asked. "Any chance?"

"Not an option at this point," I said firmly.

Just then a waitress approached our table. I was glad for the interruption; I didn't want to let memories of my sister cast a shadow on my morning.

"Hey, Conor," she said. "How are you? It's your regular time, but there's someone new at your table. And the guys look like outcasts over there. Who's your friend?"

"Hi, Violet. This is my new neighbor, Kate Lemanski. Kate, this is Violet Brewster, one of the owners of the place."

"Nice to meet you, Kate." She extended her hand in a warm greeting. I was still not used to the openness and friendliness, here. I was accustomed to the city where you always had to be on guard a little. "Hey," she said, "I knew the Lemanskis. They lived in the huge log house on the river, right? Are you Joe and Mary's daughter?"

"Yes, I am one of them," I said.

"Oh, that's right, the twins. I remember you two running around the ice cream shop when you were little. You used to come for the summer and weekends to visit your grandparents."

"Ice cream shop?" I asked.

"Yes, this used to be Brewster's Ice Cream Palace. We started having trouble in '08 when the recession hit and it became more and more difficult to keep a seasonal ice cream shop going. The tourists weren't coming as much as before, trying to save on gas and motel bills, etc. So, we looked at what the community might need, and with a name like Brewster, a coffee shop was a no-brainer," she said with a chuckle. "Anyway, I hope you'll stop by often; we have great coffee and excellent baked goods. What can I get you guys, today?"

"I'd like to try one of your blueberry muffins and a short mocha decaf, please," I said.

"You got it. Conor, the regular?"

"Yep, you know I'm a creature of habit. Thanks, Vi."

I put my chin in my hand, thinking. "I remember Brewster's Ice Cream well, but I never connected the two, because I was looking at it as a cute name for a coffee shop."

"You really don't remember, then?" asked Conor.

"Remember? What?"

"Let's see. It was the summer I was 15. I got my first job working at Brewster's Ice Cream. I was so excited and felt so grown up. One day, in walked a beautiful girl, long swinging auburn hair, hazel eyes, short shorts, and nicely tanned legs. I knew she wasn't a local; I pretty much knew everyone around. She asked for a mint chocolate chip cone. I was eager to show off my new scooping skills. As I handed it over the counter to her, the top scoop immediately flopped to the floor. I guess I hadn't anchored it well. She was so startled, she slipped on the ice cream and felt flat on her-"

"Oh, no! That was you! That's why you looked so familiar when I first met you. It really wasn't your fault, I- I," I stuttered. "Well to be honest, I was attracted to you, too, and I think I wasn't paying attention," I laughed. I blushed knowing what the next memory was going to be. Will he go there? Will he say it?

He did. "I felt so bad, so I asked if I could meet you when I was done working and take a walk down by the river with you. There was a carnival in town and there were a lot of activities going on in the park."

"I agreed," I said, "without telling my sister or my parents. But your name wasn't Conor. I would have remembered that. I've always known the name of the boy who gave me my first kiss when we were on the back side of the food tent." I blushed again as I remembered the sweet, new sensation of that kiss. "You said your name was Jack."

"That's right," he said with a sly grin. "I thought I had blown my chance with you forever with my clumsiness, and I didn't think I would ever see you again, so just in case you told someone that first I dropped your ice cream and then made a very inexperienced attempt at a kiss, I decided to use a different name."

We paused as the coffee and muffins were placed in front of us. The muffin was warm, with a little crunch on top and it was loaded with very large Michigan blueberries. My mocha decaf was chocolate coffee heaven!

"I guess that makes us old friends, then, Conor," I said softly, as I peeled off my muffin paper and looked up through my eyelashes.

He paused to take a sip of some very rich smelling coffee, and then went on to say, "I think I've figured out the rest of the story, now."

"Rest? There's more? I don't think I ever saw you again after that day. As a matter of fact, I looked for you after that whenever I was in town."

"Well," he began, "I think I may have mistaken your sister for you. I didn't know you were a twin, of course, and I saw you, or I thought it was you, at the canoe landing. I started to approach, but got a very cold look and flip of the head."

"Her signature move," I interjected.

"It was obvious the snobby girl from the city didn't want anything to do with a towny. I backed right down, then and there. The guys saw it all and laughed at me for a while, but I lived."

"Oh, I'm so sorry. My sister always was full of self-importance and thought she was better than anyone else, at that age. I wish I had never told her about my first encounter with you. She was probably jealous that I got kissed before she did. I'm sorry for your humiliation. I would not have sent you away, believe me."

"Well, that does help my teenaged, bruised ego, a little, to know that," he said. He reached out to touch my hand. His eyes had such a sparkle it was hard to concentrate. "Can I see you, again, soon, Kate? I'd really like to get to know the real Kate, the girl of my dreams."

"I'd like that, Conor." I was more than a little flustered, so I did what I always do, I left. "But right now, I'd better take off. Hoagy is waiting in the car, and I have a few more stops to make while I'm in town." I reached for the ticket that was left on the table when the coffee arrived.

"My treat," he said, looking me straight in the eyes, "I'll call soon."

Hmm, a gentleman on all fronts; it was then I made a decision that the time was not right to tell Conor about Jamie. Not yet.

I waved a quick goodbye, and walked out to my loyal Hoagy, patiently waiting for me.

⌘ Chapter Nine ⌘

Conor - 2014

After Kate left me from Brewster's, I sat for a few minutes with my hands wrapped around my coffee, reflecting back to the summer I had first met her. We'd had an immediate connection, and it was something I had felt deep in my soul. I remembered thinking as soon as I had handed her the ice cream, that I would kiss her at some point, even though at that time in my life I had never kissed a girl before. And as soon as I had accomplished what I knew was inevitable, I had forever defended the term "puppy love." That's why it was such a crushing blow when I had received the brush-off from her, or who I had thought was her. From that day on I was very careful to kiss only girls I knew would be receptive to the idea. In others words, I waited in agony until they made the first move.

Once I met Tammy, things fell easily into place. I loved her with all of my heart, but I had never had to work for her – not that she was easy, but it was just that we were so in-sync that everything happened smoothly between us, and that was the way we both wanted it. No drama, she used to say. Maybe every guy is always looking for the one he can conquer, thereby validating his manhood. I didn't think I was that way, but this need for Kate was overpowering. When I had touched her hands at the table here at the coffee shop, I felt it to my core, but I wanted to make sure it wasn't just because I had been alone for so long. Was I just imagining this strong pull toward her? I didn't think so. At this point it felt as if I had found something I had lost a long time ago, and the discovery brought me wonder and joy. I certainly was not ready to let the guys know any of this, though. I'd never live it down.

Glancing at the guys, I saw them motioning me to come over, so I decided I'd better get it over with. The inquisition was about to begin. I pushed back my chair, scraping the chair legs loudly on the floor. I wondered when the Brewsters would get around to fixing these things. The sound was annoying, especially on busy days when everyone was coming and going.

"Hey Matt, Ted, Joe." I pulled out the fourth chair, lifting it this time to avoid the screech. I threw my leg over the back and sat down. "Don't you guys have work to do? Break time must be over by now. I was just about to head back." I was hoping to avoid the questions that I knew were about to fly at me.

"We've got a few minutes left," said Matt, the foreman of our group. "Right now, we're more interested to know what went on over there. It looked pretty intense for a while."

"We were just trying to figure out how we knew each other in the past. It was a walk down memory lane," I said, trying to act casual and uninterested.

"It didn't look that way to us. You could feel the electricity all the way over here. Even Vi felt it when she delivered the coffee," piped in Ted. "She told us you two were on fire, and she could feel the vibes all the way behind the counter to the cappuccino machine."

"Were you guys watching my every move? If I had been aware of that, I would have been really uncomfortable. And I'm sure Kate would not have appreciated it much, either."

"We're just looking out for you, Conor, you know that," added Joe. "She looks special to me. If I didn't already have a wife and three kids, I might try to knock you out of the picture and make a play myself." He gave me a playful jab, as the rest of the guys laughed.

"Seriously, Conor," said Matt. "It's good to see you take an interest in someone after all of this time. We're really happy for you."

"Thanks guys, but let's take this one step at a time. This is the first chance I've really had to spend time with her, and it was only for a short time, at that."

"Then, we'd better remedy that," said Joe. "How about a picnic or something with the family?

Ask her over to meet the wives. We'll play it cool. Promise."

"Whoa, fellas. A little too soon. Can you just step back and let me do it my way? I need to ease into this thing. You know I've never had much experience dating. There's only been Tammy since high school. This is kind of a strange experience for me. And maybe nothing will develop with Kate, anyway. I don't want to move too fast."

Matt nodded to the other guys. "Okay, we'll back off. Just don't let her get away. And remember if you need anything, like a wing man, or whatever, we're there for you. We love you, man."

"Okay, it's starting to get deep in here, so now it's time to go for sure. Back to work, you idiots." All four chairs screeched at the same time, as one of them yelled, "Vi, fix these chairs!"

Later that day, when I was home alone, I thought about Kate again. Man, she sure had a grip on me. But there was Tammy's picture on the desk looking back at me. When she was looking at me like that, from the framed glass, it felt like I had been cheating and had just been caught. I remembered that we had been to the beach the day I snapped the photo. It was the first summer after our wedding; we were still newlyweds, high on life. We played and splashed in Lake Michigan all afternoon like little kids. Someone had floated a picnic table out into the water, and we dove off of it until we were exhausted. We ran across the hot sand, laughing all the way, and then we laid on our towels side by side in the burning sun and stared into each other's eyes. Tammy had the most amazing eyes, with flecks of color that spoke her love for me without ever uttering a word. She was the kind of person that always had a smile on her face. Her mother said she came out that way. It made it very easy to love her and to love being with her.

Sometimes at night, when we were in bed and the lights were out, we would talk way into the early hours of the morning going over our hopes and dreams for the future. We would often discuss friends and family, sharing who said what during the day. Tammy never had a bad word to say about anybody. If I so much as went anywhere near what she would consider gossip, she would change the course of the conversation with a kind word for that person, showing compassion for what they might be going through.

I looked deeply into the eyes in the photo wondering what she would think about the fact that I was interested in someone else. My eyes filled with tears as I remembered a conversation we had had during one of those late night talks. It was a "what if" type of talk. She had said, "What if one of us dies and leaves the other one behind? What would you do?"

"I don't want to think about that," I said. "I couldn't bear it."

"But it's something every couple should discuss," she insisted. "Okay, I'll go first then. I couldn't stand the thought that you would be left alone to grieve your life away. I would want you to marry again someday."

"How can you say that?" I asked in a shocked tone. "I'm not nearly so generous. I wouldn't want you to be miserable, but the thought of you with someone else is horrible."

"But, Conor, you wouldn't be here on Earth any longer. You would be in Heaven and you'd be very happy. Wouldn't you want the same for me?"

"Yes, I'd wish happiness and companionship for you. But could you grieve just a little while and not run to the first handsome lifeguard or hot fireman you see?"

"Silly," she laughed, "of course I would grieve. That's human nature. But eventually I'd have to go on living. I'm not saying it would be easy, but I know I would need a partner in life, and I know you would need one even more. Who would make your sandwiches for you when you are watching the game? Who would remember to buy you shaving cream? Who would wash your socks and underwear before you ran out? You'd be hopeless without someone to look after you."

"Do I really make you do all of that for me?"

"No, you don't *make* me; I do it because I love you. And if you were to find someone new, she could take over where I left off."

"I understand that. But if I die first, could you just marry for money or the convenience of having a handyman around to take care of you, and leave the sex out of it? Maybe you could be celibate for the rest of your life. Then I could deal with this little agreement you are trying to rope me into."

"Okay, it's a deal – money or practical purposes only. No sex allowed." She went into a spasms of giggles as I reached for her, pulled her into my arms, and sealed the deal.

It was funny how I could recall that night and what we had discussed almost word for word. We never brought the subject up again, because we were young and full of life. We never thought anything could ever happen to make us think about that topic again. But then it had. And because of that talk, I knew where Tammy stood. She would want me to go on, whether it was with Kate or someone else, and she would *expect* me to find someone with which to share the rest of my life. Could I do it? It would mean putting Tammy aside for a while as I concentrated on the new woman. I wasn't sure I was up for the task. Task? What was I thinking? This shouldn't be a chore. No, the chore would not be getting to know Kate; the chore would be learning how to live without Tammy on my mind 24/7. I brushed the tears from my eyes, kissed her picture and placed it in the drawer. I slowly closed the drawer, stood there a while, then opened the drawer and took it back out. No! -- I didn't get a divorce. She had died. She had left me alone to flounder like a Canada goose without its mate. I wasn't ready to put her away like a piece of paper that made a mess on the top of the desk.

I was prevented from contemplating my dilemma any further because there was a quick short knock on the door; it was the same one we had used as kids whenever we wanted to enter the other's room. I knew in an instant it was my sister, Ellen.

"Hey, Squirt, what's up?" I said, hoping she couldn't see in my eyes what I had been thinking about.

"Just thought I'd drop by and see how you're doing. I brought a few new books. I had them on hold for you at the library and they just came in. Political thrillers. You'll love this author."

"Thanks, Sis. I was out of reading material. Is that the only reason you came over?"

"Well, actually, I went over to Brewster's to get a cinnamon roll and some coffee, and Violet couldn't wait to tell me you had coffee with Kate Lemanski, that new person at the log lodge. I have to admit I was anxious to see how it went."

"Wow, news travels fast. The next time I have a date, I'll take her out of town."

"Next time? Oh, Conor, that's wonderful!"

"Yeah, well, could you just not harass me about it? I plan to take it very slow. I just dipped my toe in the dating waters today. I'm not sure how I feel about it. I won't be ready to go all the way for a long time."

"That's good enough for me. It's a start and I'm proud of you. I promise I'll stay out of your business – really I will." Ellen kissed me on the cheek and waved as she bounced out the door as quickly as she had come.

"Well, Tammy," I said out loud. "Your position on the desk is secure, for a while anyway."

⌘ Chapter Ten ⌘

Kate - 2014

It had been a very enlightening brunch. Just as always, Lily had interfered and made problems for my life. I'll bet anything she knew that Jack (Conor) was looking for me, and that he had not meant to approach her at all. She never wanted me to have anything that she didn't get first. She always said she was owed first "dibs" since she was the first-born.

I had seen Conor a few times after that, and he had turned his head away and hopped on his bike, riding in the opposite direction. It was quite a blow; my new crush had rejected me completely. For years I always thought that it had something to do with my kissing. Later, I decided that I had just been used for a young boy's experimentations. Maybe it was one of those guy-bets as to who could kiss the weekender first. I was bitter on the idea of having a boyfriend for quite a while after that.

Knowing that Lily had changed the course of

my history was nothing new. She had often decided who was best for me to date throughout high school and college, making subtle, and sometimes not so subtle, suggestions and manipulations as to who I should see. Later, I came to realize if it was someone she wanted, she steered me away from him, so she could have a clear path to him herself.

I shook my head to clear images of my sister. I was over her and done with it all. The past is the past. Conor and I had a real connection today. If something comes of it, it will happen naturally, and Lily won't be here to get in my way.

I drove down the block to drop off the Goodwill bags, then turned the car in the opposite direction, heading towards the library. The Eagle Creek Library was quite new and modern looking. A sculpture on the front lawn gave credit to the loggers of old who were the builders of this town. At one time logging was a thriving business here. Eagle Creek still held a Logger's Festival every summer to commemorate that fact. I remember attending the chainsaw carving and log rolling competitions when I was a kid. I read the plaque on the door before entering. It seemed that the whole community had come together with their fundraising, along with some sizable donations, to make this project happen.

I loved the smell of a library, especially a new one. The dark green carpet and mahogany stained wood was both tasteful and restful. I approached the circulation desk and a beautiful woman, defying all stereotypes of librarians, got up from her work station behind the glass wall. Her blue eyes were so vibrant it was startling. What was it about the blue eyes in this town? I wondered if she was used to the startled look on peoples' faces when they first saw her; she seemed completely untouched by any flattery she must have received throughout her young life. She had dark hair, swept up in a clip. I knew that style well; it was for ease at work so the hair doesn't keep falling in your face. There's nothing more aggravating than constantly having to brush your hair back while trying to shelve books.

She didn't wear the frumpy long skirt favored by most librarians, though, but instead wore a fashionably short skirt, just above the knees, and low heels. I wondered how she was able to maneuver the step stool, while reaching high for the top shelf without exposing herself. And then there was the problem of bending down low to get to the very bottom shelf, which either required a squatting position or bending at the waist, which could give patrons a nice view of a derriere, if you weren't careful. I always preferred to wear comfortable slacks and nice top with a little jewelry and makeup, thereby retaining my modesty while keeping my feminine look.

"Good morning – oh, I guess it's noon already. How can I help you?" She smiled and flashed small dimples on each side of her mouth.

"I'm new in town, and I'd like to get a library card. I just moved in a few days ago, but I can't go for very long without my library fix," I said.

"Well, we're always glad to add a new patron to our list. I'll get you a card to fill out with your information. We can get you a temporary card today and the permanent one will arrive in the mail in about a week. Of course, once you have a patron number, you can access our site online anytime for ordering books or doing research," she explained.

"Well, I have to fess up," I said. "I'm a family history librarian, – well, I was in Chicago -- so I pretty much know the drill."

"Wow, that's wonderful! We don't have a genealogy room set up yet. That's one of things we were hoping to do in the future. What did you say your name was?"

"I'm Kate Lemanski."

"Mary and Joe?"

"My parents."

"Oh, my, I knew them well. Very sweet couple. I was sad to hear about each of their deaths. It was so surprising that their passing was so close to each other. When they began staying here regularly after they retired, we saw them about once a week. They each left with a pile of books. Your mom always wanted gardening books and your dad was into old music. We ordered quite a few CDs for him. Your dad had such a sense of humor and your mother sweetly tolerated his silliness. They are really missed."

"Thank you, very much," I said, feeling a few tears well up. "It's so nice to hear those things from others about them."

"Where are my manners? I haven't told you my name yet. I'm Ellen McAuley."

I raised my eyebrows in surprise. "Any relation to Conor?"

"He's my brother," she said. And so the explanation for another pair of shockingly blue eyes; it was all in the family.

"I just had coffee with him at Brewster's."

"Oh, so you're the one," she said with a smile.

"What do you mean?"

"It's just that he's been walking on air since yesterday. I knew he had met the new person at the log lodge when he returned the key. Now that I see how gorgeous you are, I get it."

I could feel myself turn beet red again, wondering if he had told his sister about my skimpy attire at our first meeting. I don't think I have blushed this much since I was a kid. "Thank you again, that's very kind. Now to change the subject away from me, do you have computers that are available to the public here? It seems, I won't be getting service at my house any time soon."

"Too expensive, right? It's the same for a lot of folks, especially those that live off the main roads. And dial-up is so last century. That's why one of our main fundraising projects was for computers, and lots of them. We have a long row of back-to-back computers for public use right over there," she said pointing to the back near the wall. "Once you get a card, you can sign in and use it for a half hour at a time, but of course, if no one is waiting for a station, we waive that rule. We do have one rule that we have to adhere to and that is, that you must have a permanent patron card first. So I'm sorry, but you'll have to wait until it arrives before we can let you use one."

"That's okay. I understand perfectly," I said. "But I am anxious to get started on some family research. Do you have a subscription here to a

147

genealogy site?"

"We sure do, but most people here wouldn't have a clue how to use it, and honestly neither do I."

"Don't worry about it. I've been doing family research for a very long time. I would be back as soon as I get my card. I had a mystery to unravel."

Ellen studied me with steady gaze, and then a little smile slowly spread on her lips. "I'm really glad to meet you, Kate. Really glad."

"It was nice to meet Conor's sister and the librarian all at the same time," I replied.

I had filled out my personal information card while we talked, and she had already made up my temporary card, which would allow me to check out books, but I wouldn't need anything to read at this time, since I had brought several paperbacks with me. With promises to return soon, I waved and walked out the revolving door. I was truly disappointed at not being able to dig in and find out more about Jamie, today. I would just have to keep myself busy around the house until next week.

⌘ Chapter Eleven ⌘

Hattie - 1944

For several months in 1944 and 1945, I was a pretty miserable young woman. At age 16 I was expected to grow up and start acting like an adult. I thought that was exactly what I was doing the night I went to the Victory Dance with Ryan McAuley. It was the last time I would see him, and that night changed my life forever.

Our parents didn't know we were seeing each other; we had decided to keep it a secret because of our age difference. But in 1944 age didn't seem to matter to most young folks; a lot of girls were getting married at 16 and 17 to boys who had joined the service; the war had changed everything. I begged Ryan to let our folks in on it. I was sure Mama and Papa would be okay with it. I wasn't so sure about Ryan's folks, though. Ryan's father was known to hit the bottle quite a bit at certain times, but he was a real friendly guy. It was his mother I was more concerned about. I had known her ever since I was born, but she always looked at me as though she thought I was trouble, and I don't know where she got that idea. I've never been in trouble in my life. Maybe she had an intuition where Ryan and I were concerned. But I was not about to let her control my life. I was in love with Ryan; I had never felt anything this powerful in my life.

That night at the dance we had so much fun. We started out with a large group; several of the guys were leaving for basic training along with Ryan, and we had intended to have a real good time all together, but throughout the night each couple had drifted off by themselves, wanting to say a few private words to each other before it was no longer possible to be alone. Ryan and I continued to dance. It was one way we could be close.

We danced to quite a few jitterbugs and lindy hops in a row. Ryan could really go, better than most guys I knew. He was able to twist his feet the same as I did, and he would throw me over his hip and sometimes flip me over. We were quite a gymnastic pair. But then the band slowed down and we did, too. We got closer and closer with each song that the band played. Our bodies were damp from the heat; I wasn't sure if it was the temperature in the room or our own raging hormones. We decided to take a walk outside to cool off.

We talked and walked slowly as we held hands. But soon we found ourselves alone in the dark on the side of the building. As Ryan began kissing me, I knew I never wanted him to stop. I was aware at that point that this was exactly what Mama had been warning me about if I ever found myself alone with a boy I liked. She said they might want something from me that I would not want to give, and I was to be very careful. But this was different. I wanted whatever it was; I wanted to give it badly. I needed to show Ryan I loved him and he knew it. Ryan pulled me gently away from the wall of the building and led me to his car. He said we should slow down, and that we could sit in the car and talk. Ryan was so sweet. He said he wanted to write to me, and he asked if I would write back. He said he would miss me terribly, and then he started to kiss me again. It was hard to stop, but I pushed him away. I cried because he would be leaving me just when we had discovered our true feelings. How could I live through this horrible war without him? I told him I would be so worried for him, and that I would pray for him every night. I knew God would keep him safe and bring him back to me. He just had to!

I buried my face in Ryan's shoulder and cried. I think he was crying too; I heard a short sob and felt his shoulders heave. Even though he said he wanted to get over there soon and kill some Germans, I knew he was more scared than he let on. I wanted to comfort him, so I took his face in my hands and began to kiss his cheeks, then his eyes, and then his lips. That time we couldn't have stopped if there had been a bomb exploding next to us. Ryan told me he loved me over and over again, and it was all I wanted to hear for the rest of my life. I was surprised at the quick jab of pain, but Ryan stopped for a minute while I caught my breath, and then without shame or remorse, we continued. I loved him with all of my heart, and I knew now that I was truly a woman, nothing could ever be the same as before. I belonged to Ryan now and he belonged to me. We would wait out this stupid war and start a life together when he returned. We made promises that night that I never intended to go back on, but sometimes something intervenes and changes the course of your life without your permission. Neither one of us had any indication that the words we said to each other that night would be impossible to fulfill.

We knew that night was our last goodbye. Since our parents knew nothing about us, I could hardly go to the train station and give him a proper send-off. We had promised to write, but I explained to Ryan that I didn't know how I would be able to get away with it. Even if I could find money for stamps, I could hardly put them in the box at the end of our driveway. Eventually one of my parents would find out. And I didn't have a way to get into town to slip them into the corner mailbox Finally, I came up with a plan to tell Mama I was writing to Ryan as part of the volunteer war effort to keep up the morale of our soldiers. I felt guilty lying to her, but I *was* keeping up his morale, along with telling him over and over how much I loved him and missed him.

A few months later I began to feel sick whenever I smelled food, and then when I realized that I had missed two periods, I knew I had a problem. A big one. I agonized about it for days. There was no one I could trust or confide in. I knew I had to go to Mama for help. This was one thing that was not going away, and I knew she would be able to help me figure out what to do. Then we would have to face Papa.

Mama was a rock. She helped me make a plan to go visit Aunt Lucy in Traverse City until the baby was born, and then after private conversations with Papa, they decided they would adopt the baby and raise it themselves. Papa never said a bad word to me about my problem, but I know he never looked at me the same way again. I was no longer his little girl.

Through it all, I continued to write to Ryan, but I never heard from him after basic training. I wrote one-sided stories of my day, but I never told him about the pregnancy. He already had too much to think about. Getting "Jerrys" should be the only thing on his mind. Finally, I had to face the fact that he wasn't as much in love with me as I had thought. It was just like Mama had warned me about. He was just another guy who got exactly what he wanted by telling me whatever I wanted to hear. I never would have thought that Ryan was like all the rest, but I had learned my lesson well. Now it was time to move on with my life and put the past behind me. Or so I thought at the time. One thing Mama hadn't told me, was that there would now be two men in my life that I could never erase from my heart, and each time I thought of them the pain was so sharp that it cut like a knife and I thought I would die.

⌘ Chapter Twelve ⌘

Kate – 2014

I hit the button to unlock the car door. A large white head lifted to the window to greet me. "I'm back, Hoagy. Were you a good boy? Good. Let's go home." He wagged his tail as if he knew exactly what I was saying, and he was showing me that he was eager to be on our way, too.

As I arrived at my driveway, I noticed a lighter color of turned-over dirt. As soon as I began to head towards the house, I was rewarded with a nice smooth ride. All signs of ruts and grooves were gone. How nice! They had come while I was gone, just as promised. I was going to like living here permanently; everything was just so much easier. In the city whenever I had to call a plumber or electrician, I would be on the phone for hours, nagging and begging someone to come out. They seemed to be on their own schedule with no regard for their customer's needs. And once they arrived, no apologies were ever offered.

I had not had to prepay with my credit card over the phone, as I would have in Chicago; I was told they would send me a bill. So maybe that was the incentive; an eagerness to receive pay, but I was so pleased with the job they had done, I planned to call tomorrow and thank the person responsible.

Hoagy eagerly hopped out of the car, had his usual sniff and lift, and we went inside immediately. I wanted to make sure he was able to get to his water bowl if he needed it. And he did. He lapped up enough water to empty Lake Michigan, slopping most of it on the floor. Note to self: buy small rug or mat to place under dog bowls. Now, the question was what to do with my day. First, I decided, I needed to quench my own thirst, so after getting a large glass of ice water, I went back upstairs to complete the cleaning out of drawers, etc.

The log lodge had one small bedroom on the main floor, but it had most often been used as a study/office. There were four more bedrooms upstairs, one of which had been my parents'. We

157

tried, in their later years, to convince them to sleep downstairs, but they both refused to change, saying they loved the view of the river from up there.

When my great-grandfather had built the log house, the river bank was thick with trees. The story goes that there was quite an argument between my great-grandparents about clearing out some trees for a better view. My great-grandmother, or Gramma Fannie, as Lily and I called her, was dead set against cutting down trees. Great-grandpa's position was that there were so many, who would miss a few. And besides they had been logging the Michigan woods since the 1830s, one hundred years ago, and it had had no effect whatsoever on the landscape. More trees always grew to replace them, he said. She remained firm in her opinion that eventually there would be no more trees left to cut. As luck would have it, or so my great-grandfather, Grampa Bill, thought, the argument was settled for them.

One year soon after the house was built, a strong and powerful storm came through. This was well before weather surveillance and Doplar radar forecasting, so no one ever knew if it was an official tornado, but the result was that many trees were downed, exposing roots and damaging branches of near-by trees as they fell. It just so happened, that four very large pines were broken and bent in half right at the top of the bank, on the west side of the house – they were the exact same trees the argument had been about. The result was, that after cleaning up the damaged trunks, branches, and debris, a beautiful view was left from the second floor bedroom, which just happened to be my great-grandparents' room. Once Gramma Fannie was used to the idea, she agreed it was perfect, but only because God had stepped in and taken care of it Himself, thereby providing a lovely look at nature and, at the same time, settling an argument that was straining their marriage. From that point on, that room became the coveted one. As children we would race upstairs as soon as we arrived, fighting for the best view, Lily pushing and elbowing me out of the way. We often spotted deer, foxes, coyotes, wild turkeys, sandhill cranes, and eagles. When my parents took over the house, the first thing they did, was settle into that room. As soon as I was really comfortable here, I would make this my room, too, but right now it still seemed like it belonged to my mother and father, and there were memories I had to erase before I would be ready to move in. Maybe after some of their personal effects were gone, I could make it my own. A new quilt, throw pillows, different colored sheets, and some of my own trinkets and memorabilia setting out on the dresser and side tables. I was beginning to see it and feel it. Soon – soon I'd be ready.

⌘ Chapter Thirteen ⌘

Kate - 2014

Several days passed in quiet bliss. The woods
and river began to have the restorative effect on me
that I had been hoping for. I spent my evenings with
a good book, sampling various wines with Michigan
labels, and I sometimes made a fire, as the nights still
got quite cool in the late spring here. I enjoyed
pulling out a record or CD at random to see what
treasure Dad had left behind. I covered classical to
jazz to the blues, sometimes in one night. I would
jump from Ella Fitzgerald, to Tommy Dorsey, to
Billie Holiday, and then suddenly switch gears to
Rimsky-Korsakov's Scherherazade, or Ravel's Bolero.
My spirit was lifted with the sounds and tones of
sultry voices, smooth saxophones, and mournful
violins.

I spent my afternoons walking Hoagy in the
woods. At first we stayed on the path towards the
McAuley's place, but soon I felt comfortable

venturing a little away from it. As long as I could hear or see the river, I knew I would not get lost. Some areas were very familiar from my childhood. We had been allowed to roam from the large bent pine at the top of the river bank to the stone cairns, which were still in view of the second floor of the house, allowing my mother to either see us or hear our voices. No one really knows how the bent pine was formed; it may have been that a larger branch fell on it when it was a sapling, which forced the trunk to grow parallel to the ground before it decided to curve and reach for the sun, changing directions once again. Maybe someone had deliberately trained it to grow that way. However it happened, it was now the focal point of the property and the reason for the name Bent Pine Lodge. It's strong enough for two small children or even one adult to sit on, but as we quickly learned, when it begins to get warm, and the pine pitch is flowing and dripping from branches above, we would need to sit on an old blanket or towel first or you would come away with sticky pine tar on your clothing and a firm scolding from my mother.

The cairns were built by my Grampa Bill. As he was building the log house, he would unearth rocks of all sizes and toss them in a pile. Later, when the house was done, he fashioned them into beautiful works of art, stacking them so they were perfectly balanced, at various places around the property, and along the paths. While doing some research one time, I learned that cairns have been used for many purposes around the world; sometimes as burial markers, property divisions, and oftentimes, as found in this area, as trail markers. Grampa Bill's cairns all had an arrow etched into them pointing back to the house; he said it showed friends and neighbors they were welcome and marked the way if they were lost.

As Hoagy and I walked these same trails carved out and traveled by my ancestors, I felt a very real connection to the land. Their feet had walked on the same paths my feet were on now. They had experienced love and joy, loss and sorrow, pain and healing, and every other human emotion known to man. Just knowing that each one of them had come through it in one way or another was a great benefit and comfort to me. I felt I really knew these people well. They were no longer just names and dates on my family tree, but real flesh and bone. Because of them, I existed.

The ferns were beginning to get bigger now, creating a table top of green which covered the forest floor, hiding small critters and creating shade for plants that required it. I discovered jack-in-the-pulpits, trillium, may apples, and lady's slippers, and many other wild plants, growing in the deep shade of the pines or in a sunny clearing noisy with insects. I had been taught as a young child that I was only to admire, but never to cut or pull out these plants, as many were endangered species. I was told there could be huge fines levied that would be taken directly from my allowance, which was virtually non-existent most of the time. Fear of the "plant police" kept me on the straight and narrow.

I felt comfortable enough now with Hoagy to let him off the leash. He loved chasing birds and squirrels, and most of all enjoyed carrying around a big stick in his mouth, pretending in his dog's imagination that he was retrieving a newly downed duck. After our walks I would sit on the bent pine with visions of my past life swirling around in my head, but often, now, those visions would be replaced with new ones of the future, and a calmness would come over me.

Most mornings, I could be found in my mother's gardens. With my red boots, jeans, and leather gloves on, I began to clean out loose branches and dead leaves left from last year's growth. I straightened the rocks that were used as borders, and soon everything began to come to life. The daylily garden, Mother's pride and joy, was out in the clearing so it could benefit from the most hours of sun possible. Small green leaves were just beginning to emerge. If I remembered everything I had been taught, in July this garden would be a riot of color.

The wildflower garden was along the edge of the woods, receiving sun at certain times but also dappled shade throughout various times of the day as the sun moved across the sky. I looked forward to the black-eyed Susan, prairie cornflower, Shirley poppy, cosmos, and sweet Williams. The purple coneflower would produce a beautiful flower of downward tilting petals, a favorite of butterflies, and then in the fall, it would expose its seeds providing food to the finches.

The herb garden, which was started by my Gramma Fannie, was closer to the house but still in full sun, making it easy to step out of the kitchen at the back of the house and snap off some oregano or basil for the evening meal. There was a row of lavender on the edge of the herb garden, and I loved to break off a piece and walk around with it in my hands. I would lift it to my nose and inhale deeply imagining that this is what Heaven would smell like.

Soon my back was aching, screaming at me that it was time to take a break. I stood, arched a little, and then began to gather up my gardening tools. Hoagy got up from his nap in the sun to follow me once again. Sometimes I felt guilty with my movements around the yard and house, because I knew he would feel it was necessary to come with me, but he never seemed to mind; he took his duties and loyalty very seriously. I put everything back in my mother's potting shed, making sure it was all in its proper place. She loved having her own little building, and always kept it neat so she could find anything she wanted instantly. I had enjoyed using her gardening tools this past week. I had also been using my grandmother's small garden cart, which was perfectly balanced on two wheels. Her 1940s version of a lady's wheelbarrow was so perfectly balanced you could pull it with one finger, even when fully loaded. The old green paint on the metal sides was faded and worn with the orange lettering of Jackson Deluxe Cart still showing through.

There's something very intimate about using a tool, or wearing a piece of jewelry, that has belonged to a family member. It's almost like feeling their hands on yours, touching you through the article you are holding. I felt Grandma's warm hands wrapped around mine, guiding my way, as I wheeled the cart to the shed, and I knew she was happy that I was continuing to work in her and my mother's gardens.

I went inside, took off my boots, and washed up. As I passed the old record player, I popped on a 78 RPM of Nat King Cole, his soft velvety voice filling the room, as he sang Nature Boy. I poured myself a tall glass of iced tea, and fed Hoagy. By that time the record was already finished, making its scratchy noise as the turntable continued to go round and round as the needle bounced uselessly, which was the trouble with single play records; they needed a lot of attention. I looked over the CD collection, and found just what I was looking for -- Mozart. His piano, violin, and clarinet concertos were my favorites; they were so relaxing that they were oftentimes used to lull babies to sleep.

I was suddenly feeling very tired myself as the music began to relax me. The leather groaned and squeaked as I settled into the couch. I laid back, propped up my feet, and put my head on the pillow. It must have been only seconds before I fell asleep, and I had no idea how long I was out before I heard a knock on the door and Hoagy's quick short bark, announcing the arrival of company. I sat up and tried to clear my head before going to the door. I don't know why, but I am always embarrassed when caught sleeping during the day. A glance in the mirror showed a small twig sticking out of my hair, and a smudge on my cheek. I did a quick finger comb, and used my own spit on my face. Oh, boy, I was really becoming just like my mother now. Since no one else had come to my door unannounced except Conor, I wondered if it might be him again. My heart took a crazy lurch at the thought of seeing him once more. We had not talked since the day we had coffee, but instead, upon opening the door, I was pleasantly surprised to find Ellen, Conor's sister, standing there.

"Oh, hi," I said, startled to see the local librarian on my doorstep.

"I hope it's okay that I just stopped by without calling first," she said. "I wanted to bring you this instead of mailing it. I know you didn't want to wait too long." She extended the permanent library card I had been waiting for.

"Thank you, so much," I said gratefully.

"Would you like to come in? Have some iced tea, maybe, since you came all the way out here?"

"I wouldn't want to intrude."

I laughed at the formality which seemed totally out of place, here. "Of course, you wouldn't be intruding! I never have company, and I've been getting a little tired of one-sided conversations with my dog. Come in, please, that is if you have time, of course."

"Sure, I'd love to. I have always admired your home. It would be lovely to see the inside. It's so beautiful from the river."

"Well, come, then, and sit. I'll get you a glass and refill my own. Let's sit at the table where we can look out over the water. Do you boat or fish a lot that you've seen the house from the river?"

"No, my fiancé is a big fisherman, but it doesn't thrill me too much. I have gone with him on occasion just to keep him company, but I usually take a book to occupy myself; otherwise, he says I talk too much," she said as she cocked her head and shrugged her shoulders. "I don't think I do. I've never been one of those non-stop talkers like some women are, but it seems to be too much for him. Funny, though, how he enjoyed it when we were first dating!" She laughed. "I've mostly been able to see your place, though, when we go tubing."

"Oh, I had forgotten all about that. We used to do it when I was little. The whole family would go down the river at the same time with all the tubes tied together. It was so much fun."

"You'll see them floating past on weekends as soon as the weather gets better. The trouble is it has gone from a family outing to R-rated entertainment for some. Eagle Creek authorities and the River County Sheriff Department have to patrol constantly for drunks and flashers. Most of the locals don't even want to go anymore; the weekenders are ruining it for us," she said disgustedly.

"That's too bad. Seems like I read something about it in the papers, now that you mention it."

"It's just one of the few down-sides to river living. The rest is pure pleasure," she said. Ellen hesitated, bit her lip, in what I would come to know as a regular habit of both her and her brother's when they are uncomfortable. She took a deep breath and said, "There is another reason, besides delivering the library card, that I stopped by, – well, two actually."

"Oh, what is that? You look uneasy. Please feel free to speak openly."

"The first one isn't difficult to ask, so I'll start there." Ellen suddenly smiled a Cheshire cat grin. "I've had the most wonderful idea. Are you interested in a job? I mean, you never mentioned wanting to work in a library again, but I had the feeling you were just taking a break."

"I had thought about putting my resumé out there, once I was settled in and had taken at least a month off, but I never dreamed there would be an opening so close to home. Is there?" I asked.

Ellen went on to explain the idea she had recently come up with. "I was thinking about this after you left. The library board wants a genealogy room. We have the space but no one really knows what to do with it. Some of the volunteers have tried to collect books on local history, etc, so we have them on a shelf with their Dewey Decimal numbers assigned but that's as far as we've gone with it. If I can convince them to bring you on, you would have complete control of that area, and once hired and trained in our system, you would have total access to the computers. All librarians have their own key, so you can even come in before work or stay after hours to work on your own time on your research in uninterrupted silence."

"Wow, that's more than I could hope for. Is the board financially able to hire another librarian on staff? It sounds like this is an idea that has not occurred to them yet."

"Yes, we have the money. We have a very generous donor in the area, and the township just raised the designated library taxes to help cover costs that are not covered with the donation. All I'd need is your resumé. I'll take it to the library board meeting next Monday and if you are approved, then it has to go before the township board. I'm sure you'll pass with flying colors with your experience. What do you think?"

"Yes, yes. I'd love to do it!" And with that she jumped up and gave me a big hug.

Then her eyes clouded over a little. "Now, to the next reason I am here," she said quietly. "It's about Conor."

"Is he okay?"

"Sure, he's fine. Maybe I'm being overly dramatic – another flaw my fiancé accuses me of – but Conor is my brother and I am somewhat protective of him."

"Go ahead," I said. I was curious now as to where this was headed.

Ellen tossed her lovely dark hair and swiped a loose strand away from her face before speaking. "I'm not sure how much you know about Conor."

"Not much at all, except we share a love of music and we knew each other briefly when we were young."

"Conor is not complicated at all," she said. "I know I'm prejudiced, but he is a kind and generous man. He's also very easily hurt, especially after what happened. He doesn't talk about himself much, so I was sure he wouldn't go into details about his life. I decided to take it upon myself to fill you in. You see, he was married about five years ago.

"Two years after they were married, his wife, Tammy, was driving on a dark road, swerved to avoid a deer, and slammed head-on into a tree. She was killed instantly. Her best friend was with her, but she survived. Losing her was devastating for Conor. For a long time we didn't think he would ever come out of it. Dad and I did everything we could think of to encourage him to socialize. I knew he wasn't ready to date again, so I left that subject alone. I never can stand it when I see people try to set someone up with a blind date, knowing they are not ready. I feel each person has their own way and time of grieving." Ellen's eyes filled with tears as she remembered the past. "We just wanted him to attend family gatherings and meet with his buddies after work again. Maybe go to a movie. He wouldn't have anything to do with it. Finally, after a year had passed, he began to go to the coffee shop with his friends again and we saw him smile and then heard laughter once in a while. It's been three years now and he has started to come around, but still there has been no interest in anyone new – until you."

"Me?" I was surprised and, I had to admit, more than a little pleased. "We've only had a few chats and coffee once. Very casual."

"Yes, but for Conor, that is really something," she said. "I guess, what I am trying to say is that I don't want him to get hurt. If you have no interest in him, please find a way to let him know gently. It took a lot of courage for him to ask you to meet him at Brewster's that day. I felt like you were someone I could tell about his past, and you would understand."

"Actually, I completely understand, more than you know. I was married, too. It didn't end in death, but divorce. I was finally getting over that pain, when another major upset came along and hit me in the gut." I was surprised at myself for revealing this much. I am usually such a private person, but Ellen was very easy to talk to, or maybe it was just that, other than Cara, I had not been able to confide in anyone else. Then I smiled at her and said, "So you see, I have total empathy for him, and I have no intention of letting him down, anyway, because I would very much like to see him again. As a matter of fact, I was wondering why I hadn't heard from him. Just last night, I was contemplating finding an excuse to call him over," I laughed.

"That's a relief. But he's out of town on a construction job so he's been gone since Wednesday. Give it a few days. When he comes home, he might make an excuse of his own. Now, let's keep this talk between the two of us. He would kill me if he knew I had said anything about him. I just came by to give you the card and ask about hiring you, right?"

"Exactly. Mum's the word."

"Well," she said as she rose and carried her glass to the sink, "I'd better get going. Pop doesn't know where I am. He worries sometimes." I walked her to the door.

"Stop by again, Ellen, whenever you like. No need to call first."

"Thanks, I will. I enjoyed our talk. Just send your resumé to the library addressed in care of me, and I'll let you know what happens. It could take a while because the meetings are only once a month. Everything moves slowly in a small town!"

"That's fine. I'm enjoying my time off."

"Great, well, bye now." She gave Hoagy a pat on the head, and left me with a smile on my face, a new found friend, and a few things to think over – the possibility of a new job, and the fact that maybe Conor really does want to see me again.

⌘ Chapter Fourteen ⌘

Ryan - 1944-1945

Basic training was more difficult than I thought. Growing up in Western Michigan with trees, lakes, and wildlife around me everywhere, I was taught at an early age how to fish and hunt. All of my friends knew how to use a gun. We had been taught to respect and take care of weapons. But they were to be used on animals, and then only in the proper season, with a proper license. Of course, we did our share of shooting at birds with BB guns, and I guess I'm not proud of that, but it was the way we learned. I never knew anyone who had abused their right to own a gun. Now, I was being trained to kill people – human beings. I had to block the thought out of my mind that those same people had families – children, wives, parents, and girlfriends. They carried pictures in their wallets, too, and thought about getting home every night before they fell asleep. Now I was being asked to end their lives with the M1 carbine that had been assigned to me.

Some of the guys were real eager to get over there and just start shooting. I don't think they really knew what they were preparing to do. It would be difficult for me at first, but I also knew that once I was there, and I was being fired at, I would shoot back, no doubt about it. And then, once I had lost a few friends, I guess the hate would build, and I would be talking just like the rest of the guys, about the "Jerrys" and the "Krauts." My ancestry on both sides was Irish all the way back, but I knew plenty of guys from my hometown who were of German descent, their parents or grandparents had been immigrants. They all knew that they could very well be shooting at their own cousins. But we had no choice. That crazy man, Hitler, had to be stopped at all costs.

I wrote to Hattie as much as possible. I got a few letters back while I was still at Fort Benning, and then they stopped. I thought maybe her parents didn't like her writing to me, so I asked my mother to be the go-between and pass my letters on. I didn't tell my mother how much I loved Hattie, but I think she knew. She had always been close to the Bauer family, so I didn't think there would be a problem, but since I wasn't there to explain my intentions to marry Hattie when I got back, I had to admit to being a little worried as to how the families were going to take it. I personally couldn't wait to be the one to join the McAuleys and the Bauers together.

After basic training, my unit, the 10th Armored Division, Company C, was sent to Europe by way of ship. We were all concerned with where we would land and what would be waiting for us when we got there. The only way to pass the time when we weren't on duty was to play cards. A lot of the guys gambled, thinking there was a possibility they might not return so they didn't worry if they lost everything they owned. I tried to keep a positive attitude, because I was one lucky guy – I had a drop-dead, gorgeous girl to go home to.

We landed on Normandy Beach, but it was well after the first invasion and the big battle had been fought there. The guys were all silent when we disembarked our boats. It was like walking on hallowed ground. I couldn't imagine the Hell this place had been only a few months earlier. I would soon find out what Hell was, and I knew if I ever got home safely, I would do everything in my power to prevent anything like this from happening to my family ever again.

Neither Hattie nor I owned a camera, so I didn't even have a picture of her, but when I wrote to my mother, I asked if she could find a way to get me one. It didn't matter, though, if I had one or not, because her beautiful face was etched in my brain. Every night, when we made camp, and I rolled out my blanket and laid on the cold hard ground, I warmed myself with the pictures in my mind of Hattie laughing, and dancing, and the way her face lit up when she was telling me something exciting. I especially liked to think about kissing her and hearing her sweet sighs when I took her in my arms as we made love for the first and only time. One time was not enough, it would never be enough, but it was all that we were allowed before I had to serve my call to duty. I would always be crazy about her – I knew it in my bones. So I just had to get home so we could get married and start a family like the rest of the world.

Little did I know the day I first embarked on Normandy Beach what would happen to my life in the next 13 months. It was something I would never be able to erase from my memory; I could only shelve it away and try not to think about any of it, until it came crashing back when a car back fired or sharp thunder cracked across the skies. When the lightening lit up the sky on a hot summer night, I would forever be taken back to foxholes and bombs. Whenever I heard a siren, I would immediately think it was an air raid siren, and on the few times I was in an emergency room with one of my kids with a broken arm or cut, I would always remember the blood of my fallen brothers scattered on the ground. For years gently fallen snow was a reminder of crossing Germany in a blizzard without the proper clothing or boots.

When I was captured by the Germans, and taken to a POW camp, I actually thought, for a few minutes, that at least I would no longer be required to pull a trigger on another human being, but I soon learned that I would do anything to have a gun in my hands again, so I could shoot every last animal who was in a German uniform keeping me here.

Letters were rarely delivered to Stalag XII in Wiesbaden, my home away from home, and I didn't know if anyone in Michigan knew if I was alive or not. We were each given one blanket and were left on our own in a barracks type building called Quonset huts. We had no heat, so we were cold and wet all the time; shoes and socks were a luxury. We were given one meal a day, and even then we were only fed sparingly with slop that sometimes contained maggots. Each and every one of us, dropped at least 40 pounds. By the time the war was over, I was a skeleton of my old self.

When we were finally freed by our American buddies, we were sent back to camps and hospitals to get cleaned up, and we received proper meals and medications. I did everything they told me to do so I could get healthy enough to be discharged and sent home quickly. Yes, I wanted to see my mother, father, and sister, but my main goal was to get back to Hattie. I hadn't heard from her in almost a year. Would she still be waiting? In my heart I knew she would be. We had a real connection; I had always felt it. I had felt it all the way across the ocean; it was the only thing that had kept me going for those horrible months when the Germans were relentless.

And now finally, I was on my way. Mom and Pop were meeting me at the train station in Grand Rapids. I knew she would be with them. I couldn't wait to pick her up in my arms and twirl her around until we were both dizzy. First, we would spend some time alone, and then we would go dancing and spin and dip the night away. When we were exhausted and needed some fresh air, I was going to ask her to marry me, and if she would have me, I would take her dancing every Friday night for the rest of our lives.

As the train came to the station and began to slow down, I strained to see who was waiting for me. There were so many people it was difficult to find my folks. All the other fellas had someone waiting for them, too. I finally spotted my mother and father. Mom was waving her handkerchief and crying at the same time. Dad had his hat in his hand and was holding it in the air in order to get my attention. And Hattie was -- where was Hattie? I looked around frantically, and called, "Hattie!" It was then I knew. I knew it in my heart and by the look in my mother's eyes. Hattie would never be there for me. I wished I had never come home. I wished I would have been left rotting on the ground somewhere in Europe like so many of my buddies had been. And then the words to our favorite song came back to haunt me.

I'll be seeing you,
In all the old familiar places,
That this heart of mine embraces
All day through.

In that small café,
The park across the way,
The children's carousel,
The distant trees, the wishing well.

I'll be seeing you,
In every lonely summer's day,
In everything that's light and gay,
I'll always think of you that way.

I'll find you in the morning sun,
And when the night is through,
I'll be looking at the moon,
But I'll be seeing you.

⌘ Chapter Fifteen ⌘

Kate - 2014

The next day I was finally able to get my thoughts zeroed in on the "Jamie" issue. I knew I wouldn't feel satisfied until I had discovered what happened to him, thereby, fulfilling my grandmother's request. So I sat at the table with my bagel and cream cheese, and a yellow legal pad in front of me. I needed to make detailed notes to take to the library, so I could begin to dig into some public records. If my dates and places were not accurate, the research would be that much more difficult. I realized after I had gotten home from the library that my family tree was on my laptop and I didn't need Internet to access it. I could also take the laptop to the library and use their WiFi, thereby avoiding the use of their computers and the allotted time limit restriction. I had a subscription to a family tree research site already. What had I been thinking? I could have been working on this days ago! So much for my detail-oriented librarian brain. Maybe I had sabotaged myself purposely because I wasn't ready yet. It wasn't until my housecleaning and yard work was complete, that I felt comfortable spending time digging into names and dates of the past.

First, I made a rough sketch of the direct line of descendants, with plenty of space next to each name for notes.

Mary Katherine Lemanski, born June 1, 1974

Lily Ann Lemanksi, born June 1, 1974

Parents:

Mary Klein Lemanski, born 1954

Joseph Edward Lemanski, born 1950

Grandparents:

Sophia Bauer Klein, born 1936

Carl Hans Klein, born 1931

Great-Grandparents:

Frances Schuster Bauer, born 1910 Germany

Wilhelm Frederick Bauer, born 1909

Children:

Hattie, born 1928 (my great-aunt)

Sophie, born 1936 (my grandmother)

James, born 1945 (Hattie's child with Ryan McAuley)

And now for the McAuleys which I knew little about, going only on what was written in the letter and what I remembered from my childhood.

Conor McAuley, born approx. 1972?

Ellen McAuley (Conor's sister)

Parents:

Eric McAuley, born ?

Conor's mother's name, unknown, born?

Grandparents:

Ryan McAuley, born? (father of Jamie with Hattie)

Roma, (Ryan's wife) maiden name, unknown, born?

Children with Roma:

Eric and Cindy (both half-siblings to Jamie)

Okay, things were a little clearer now. One of my concerns had been how these relationships would affect Conor and me. I certainly did not want to get into the same complicated mess as Jamie and Cindy had. A closer look showed me that Jamie is Conor's grandfather's son, in other words, his half-uncle.

Sophie is my grandmother and Hattie, her sister, is my great-aunt. So Jamie is Sophie's nephew and my mother's cousin. That makes him my second cousin. So my second cousin, Jamie, is Conor's half-uncle. I think we're safe if anything is to go forward between Conor and myself. All in the family, maybe, but far enough removed not to worry about, but it sure complicates things. Will it matter to him? I'll have to find a way to bring it up. It will give me a good excuse for our next meeting, if I need one. He might also be able to ask his father about some details I'll have to have in order to keep my search for Jamie moving forward.

Energized and ready to get started, I gathered my laptop, notes, and pens. Hoagy would have to stay behind for the first time since I got him. I'm sure he wouldn't be happy, but I would not leave him in the car for what might be hours.

"Guard the house, Hoagy. On guard." As soon as I gave the command, his ears perked up, and he took a position by the door, flopping down heavily on a rug. Wow, that was easy. "Good boy."

It was another perfect day; the air was exactly skin temperature, producing a sense of well-being. I rolled down my car windows; there was no need for the A/C, and I felt the warm breeze on my face. I hoped I would never get used to the fresh, clean air which was so comfortable to breathe here. The low humidity was surprising with all of the lakes and rivers in the area, but I suppose the constantly moving air kept it under control. It's funny how when you are a child none of these things are even noticeable; you just take each day as it comes and deal with it at that time. Now, I watch the weather closely, planning my outings and events around it, and following the weather is crucial to my gardening plans.

The drive to the library was quick and easy now that I knew where I was going. I got my things from the car and walked clumsily to the building, trying to balance both my carry case and my purse.

Laptops are lighter than they used to be, but at 7 pounds, they have a long way to go. It might be time to spring for a lighter weight notebook. I glanced around, looking for Ellen, but saw no one at the desk, so I headed for the tables near the back. I was pleased to see they were plug-in ready just in case my battery went dead.

I was starting to get excited now that I was finally ready to begin my research. It was always like this for me, even when I was working on something for someone else and had no connection whatsoever to the family. I loved the hunt!

The computer was booted up now and ready to go, so I clicked on my ancestry search site. I had to think for a moment as to where to start. Jamie was born in 1945 so he would not show up on a census until 1950. Unfortunately, the 1950 census won't be available to the public until 2022, because of the 72-year rule which provides privacy protection. No doubt it was made for cases just like this one. Shoot, that means I have to find another route. Maybe a Michigan death record search.

"Hey, you look intense."

I jumped, the sound of a voice jarring me out of my deep concentration.

Ellen laughed. "Oh, I'm sorry. I didn't mean to startle you."

"Oh, no, that's quite all right. I just go into another mode when I'm working on my family tree. I block everything out and hear nothing around me at all."

Ellen pointed to my laptop and said, "I see you're using your own computer."

"Yes, I don't know what I was thinking. I might as well use your WiFi and save the library computers for someone else," I said. "Besides, I have my whole family tree loaded on this so it's easy to refer to."

"Well, I'll leave you to your work. I just came over because I spotted you over here, and I wanted to invite you to our book club. We meet on Wednesday night at 7:00. If you're interested the book list is at the checkout desk. You're a little late for this month's book, but you could still stop by and meet everyone."

"Thank you, that sounds like something I'd like to do. I think maybe I'll wait, though, until I can read the next book. I'd feel more comfortable if I had something to contribute to the discussion."

"No problem!" And there were those dimples again as her whole face lit up with her radiant smile. "I have your phone number in the file, so okay if I send you a reminder text?"

"Perfect," I said. "But I'm sure I'll see you again before then. If not here, then maybe we can grab coffee?"

"I was hoping you might be interested in that," she said. "Let's make a pact that we won't let anything interfere with our new friendship, even Conor." She raised an eyebrow, obviously hoping for something new from me to report.

I had nothing to offer so I just said, "I'd like that very much."

Ellen glanced over at her desk and saw a line starting to form. "I'd better get back to work; we'll talk later," she said with a quick little wave goodbye.

Okay, so now where was I? No census, okay –

try death records. Death records are considered public information so no matter when you die, your record can be accessed. I first typed in James Bauer, which was the name he grew up with. Everyone who appeared was either too old or too young. Then I tried James McAuley, thinking he might have changed his name to the surname of his father once he knew his real parentage. I couldn't enter a middle name, since I had no idea what it might be. I wish I had been more thorough when I first started my family tree. Of course, I was young then, and had no idea where my ancestry would take me. Note to self: Go back to the immediate family records and acquire as many birth and death records as possible.

The search brought up three James McAuleys in Michigan who were born in 1945. There was a James W. who had died in 1946 - no, he would only be one year old at the time of his death. Then there was a James R. who had died in 1967 – a possibility. And a James D. who had passed away in 2000 at the age of 89 – too old. On a hunch I went for the James R. Could it be that R stood for Ryan? A click on his name showed that when he passed away his legal residence was Traverse City. That was more than a coincidence since my James was born in Traverse City. The online record at this point showed nothing more than name, date, and place of death. Maybe Jamie had gone back to visit Aunt Lucy. He would have met her on occasion at weddings and funerals or maybe a family trip to visit his "mother's" sister. Or was he on a quest to search for his birth record? It would have been filed in Grand Traverse County. If I requested an actual death record from the County, I could glean more information. My gut told me this was the one. If so, once I got the death record, I could determine the internment site and also request the birth record after that. I'd like to believe my grandma, but what if she was wrong. She was just a young girl, after all. It's always best to check the facts carefully. If I had done more digging when I was 20, I would have known all of this already. But there had been no reason to question the facts I was given by my grandmother at that time. I checked the city directory records also but there wasn't anything listed for a James R McAuley. He might have been living in a neighboring town, or just outside the city limits, at that time, so the place of residence would not be listed in the Traverse City book. It seems as though Jamie was one of those caught in between the cracks where genealogy research is concerned. This was not going to be easy. I just hoped it wouldn't be one of those "brick walls."

I decided to send an email request for the death record. I was allowed to use my debit card for the purchase. There was a ten dollar research fee, but I was more than willing to pay. I would receive something in about a week. So once more, the waiting game begins.

⌘ Chapter Sixteen ⌘

Kate - 2014

It was Wednesday of my second week here. I sometimes looked backed on my life in Chicago and remembered all of my friends and social activity. Life was quite different now, and I often felt loneliness creep over me. Of course, long talks with Cara in the evenings helped, and meeting Ellen was a bonus. I felt I had at least one friend in both cities. And then there was Conor. What exactly was he to me? A handyman? A neighbor? My friend's brother? Maybe he was just an acquaintance, and that's all that would come from that relationship. But I knew I wanted more and since I had not heard from him since our coffee time at Brewster's, I decided to take the matter into my own hands. Sometimes a girl's gotta do what a girl's gotta do. I shot out a quick text asking if he might want to come over for dinner on Friday night. My fingers shook as I hit the send button. Was he that important to me? Or was it just because it had been such a long time since I had taken the initiative with a man? Okay, deep breath, it's done, and as my mother used to say "Que Sera, Sera." She would dance me around the floor, whenever I asked a question about my future, and she would sing:

When I was just a little girl
I asked my mother
What will I be?
Will I be pretty?
Will I be rich?
Here's what she said to me.
Que sera, sera
Whatever will be, will be
The future's not ours to see
Que sera, sera
What will be, will be.

I'll just have to take my mother's, and Doris Day's, advice, and relax, and wait for a return text, if it ever comes.

Surprisingly, his text showed up immediately. "Thanks for the invite. I was just thinking of U. Finishing up a job in St. Joe. Planned on asking U 2 dinner when I got back. Yes, would love 2 come. Time? I'll bring wine."

"C U at 7:00 p.m. 2 late for a Michigander?"

"I can handle it. :)"

I wrapped my arms around myself, while I danced and twirled around the floor, singing Que Sera Sera. There it was, happiness! It was beginning to feel familiar.

In order to keep busy, I spent Thursday in the library again, looking through cemetery records in the Traverse City area. It was difficult not knowing what part of the city Jamie had lived in and if there was a church affiliation. I had to systematically look through the records for each cemetery in the county. Quite often a person is not interred near their home but in a family plot or someplace with less expensive fees than the local cemetery, so I tried to put myself into the situation. Was there family, perhaps a wife, left behind to bury him? If so, who and where were they?

Suddenly, I got a hit on the Old Mission Cemetery, in Grand Traverse County. Grand Traverse Bay is divided into the West and East Arm by the Old Mission Peninsula, and that's where the cemetery was. Yes, the date of birth for James R. McAuley was accurate to what I knew as his birthday. This James had died on April 28, 1967 just before his 22nd birthday. It most likely was my Jamie. Now that I had a date and place, I could begin to scour newspaper obituaries.

After checking the Internet for publications in the area, I found The Traverse City Record-Eagle was listed as a newspaper for that time period. I then discovered a link to the obituary records and typed in a date range of two weeks after April 28, 1967, allowing time for the death notice to appear. At first, being totally wrapped up in the hunt, I was excited at getting a hit, and then my heart sank as the realization set in that Jamie was actually dead. I was hoping to meet and talk with him and tell him he still had family who cared. He would have only been 69.

I had hoped I would discover he had lived a good long life. I felt tears fill my eyes when I read the obit.

Corp. James R McAuley of Foxtrot Co., 2nd Battalion, 1st Marine Regiment succumbed to wounds suffered in battle on April 28, 1967, at the Que Son Valley in Viet Nam. Corporal McAuley was born on November, 17, 1945 in Traverse City, Michigan. He is survived by his aunt, Lucy Bauer, of Leeland. A private funeral will be held on May 16, 1967 allowing time for the remains to be transferred to Michigan.

I sat back, took a deep breath, and said a silent prayer for Jamie, who had given his life for our country. There were questions I would probably never have the answers to. Did Aunt Lucy ever notify Hattie that her son was with her? Apparently she had not told my grandmother, her own sister, and certainly Ryan had not been informed. It seems Jamie had died in the world alone with no one but a great-aunt to care for his remains.

Friday evening came quickly. I had cleaned and cooked all day. I decided a solid Italian meal of spaghetti and meatballs would probably hit the spot with Conor. Besides, it was one of my specialties. Even though my mother came from a German background and my father was Polish, she loved to experiment with ethnic foods. She had discovered a spaghetti sauce recipe that was a favorite of all her guests. I had been making it for years and always had the same results. I made large, man-sized meatballs with Parmesan and herbs added in the meat, then I placed them in the broiler on low. The spaghetti sauce had been slowly simmering; the smells of garlic, oregano, and fresh tomatoes filled the air. I knew there would not be time to bake my own bread, so I had picked up a beautiful loaf at the bakery in town. It never failed to surprise me what wonderful baked goods I could find here. I sliced the loaf open, spread olive oil on it and popped it in the oven. As soon as it came out of the oven, I rubbed a clove of garlic over the hot toasted bread. Earlier I had made a dipping sauce with olive oil and Italian herbs which had been grown in my mother's garden, then dried. The pasta was almost ready. I was hoping he would be on time or all would be ruined

I dressed casually, sensing that it was what he would prefer, choosing a salmon colored top to compliment my auburn hair and hazel/green eyes. The deep-cut vee gave just enough glimpse of cleavage to be enticing. I filled in the bare chest space with a new necklace I had purchased at a local North Woods artisan/gift shop. I felt good about my selection, and I hoped he would appreciate it, too.

I was quite nervous because I had decided I had no choice but to fill Conor in on all of my findings on his family – and mine. And I needed to find just the right time to bring it up. There was a knock on the door and my heart started to pound, more out of excitement this time than nerves. The steam from the kitchen had made my face a little damp, so I quickly grabbed a kitchen towel and patted myself down. A glance in the mirror showed my makeup was still perfectly applied. Okay, here goes. When I opened the door, I was shocked once again by those blue eyes, as I was each and every time I had ever seen him. We grinned at each other for a few minutes like school kids, awkwardly greeting each other at the front door as they were about to go to the Prom.

"Come in. You're right on time," I said, composing myself and going into hostess mode.

"Hi, Kate." Conor stepped forward, handed me a small bouquet of jonquils and tulips, and leaned in for a kiss on my cheek. "I knew you liked flowers," he said. "I hope you're not allergic to these; I wasn't sure what you would like."

"They're beautiful and some of my favorites! Thank you so much. Make yourself at home, while I get these in a vase."

He had the most beautiful smile a man ever had, with the same dimples as his sister, but with the scars added there was a ruggedness that was very appealing. "Wow, something sure smells great!"

"I hope you like Italian," I said. "It's just basic spaghetti and meatballs."

He touched his stomach and said, "I never turn down an Italian meal."

"Would you like wine or beer tonight?"

"I think I'll stay with the theme and have a glass of wine with you. Can I open and pour for you?"

"Sure. That would be nice. Thank you. Here are the glasses. I'll just finish plating this up and then we can talk over our dinner."

He lifted an eyebrow. "Oh, is this a business meal?" He looked a little disappointed.

"Oh, no, I'm sorry," I said. "I just meant that we have a lot to learn about each other. But now that you bring it up there is something that I need to discuss with you. We can save that part for later, though."

"Oh, good," he said, with a deep look into my eyes. "I was hoping this was more of a first date."

There's that heart lurch again. I lowered my eyes and then looked back. "Yes, I guess it kind of is."

He nodded. "Good. I've been looking forward

to our first date since the minute I first saw you when I came to return the key. As soon as you opened the door, I wanted to know more."

Was it my imagination, or was there a slight emphasis on the word "saw"? I was so flustered I could think of nothing to say but, "Okay, then, dinner's ready." How stupid was that? He must have thought I was an idiot. You sure could tell I was out of practice. I hadn't flirted with a man in a very long time.

We walked into the dining area, and Conor actually came around and pulled out the chair for me! Now, that was something I had not expected. He was proving to be a man full of surprises. Good looking and a polished gentleman.

"So, Conor, tell me about yourself."

"Hmm, where would you like me start? I was born and raised right here in River County, in the house next door, as a matter of fact. I went to Eagle Creek High School and then to Michigan State for my engineering degree. I always loved construction of any kind, and now I own my own business. As far as personal, I guess Ellen told you about me already."

I looked up quickly from my plate. "She said it was to be our secret. I'm surprised she told you she brought it up with me."

"We're very close," he said. "We don't keep much from each other for too long. She said she started to feel guilty that she had gone behind my back and discussed personal issues. Frankly, I'm glad she did, so I don't have to talk about it with you. Now, you know, and we can move on from there."

"I am so sorry for what you went through. I'm sure it was a very difficult time."

"Thank you, it was. Now enough about me. This is a fantastic meal, by the way." I nodded my thanks as he went on, "Let's move on to you. I know nothing except that you visited your grandparents here and then once your parents owned the house, you came up regularly in the summer."

"Well, I'll start at the beginning and try to keep it short. I was actually born in St. Joe and raised in Benton Harbor. You already know that I have a twin and you have first- hand experience with how she could manipulate my life."

"You said, 'could.' I take it you set her straight, at some point, then?"

"Yes, in more ways than one. We don't speak anymore. And that actually leads to the part of my life story that is not so pleasant, for me anyway. Are you sure you want to hear?"

"Of course, I want to know everything about you. But only if you feel comfortable telling me."

I was a little nervous about this part, because I didn't want to get emotional and scare him away, but it was time I started to talk more about it, and Conor seemed like a compassionate man. I felt I could share anything with him.

⌘ Chapter Seventeen ⌘

Lily ~1994

"Kate, I don't know what is wrong with you. Every time we get invited to a frat party, you won't go. Don't you want to be popular?"

"Lily, that's so high school. I'm really not interested in getting drunk until I throw up and going home with someone I barely know. That's your style, not mine."

Kate had her nose in a book once again. That's how she had been since we were kids. Always the party-pooper. I just couldn't be bothered with her anymore. I had promised Mom and Dad that we would stick together at college, but she just wasn't any fun, and a girl had to have her fun.

College was the ultimate freedom for me. There were so many people to meet and there were loads of new guys on which to practice my feminine charms. It seemed I had been waiting for this time of my life forever. The girls would be here soon to pick us up, and twin or no twin, I was going to that party. I rather liked being in groups without Kate, anyway. We were identical mirror-image twins. Our family and close friends could tell us apart easily, but new people always got us confused.

Sometimes Kate would meet a new guy, and he would assume I was her or vice versa. I loved to pretend that I was Kate for a while, and then I would show him a new side to her sweet personality. He might have thought Kate was a respectable girl, someone he could take home to his mother, but when I got through with him, he couldn't believe how she had become a "bad girl" overnight. I'd crawl all over him, and show him a real good time, and of course he loved it, but that visit home to Mama was never brought up again. Then the next time he actually went out with Kate, she couldn't figure out why he was so aggressive. She'd be all indignant, calling him a jerk, and then she'd drop him. It was such fun! For some odd reason, Kate never caught on to my little game.

One day, though, I was laughing with Tanya about Kate being such a goody-two-shoes, and Kate overheard us. She was really hurt that I would talk about her behind her back. I felt bad for about two seconds. She deserved to know what other people thought about her. Sister or not, I was not going to let her bring my standing on campus down. Kate was so kind and sensitive that she just couldn't help being good. When I would come back from a "date" and complain about the treatment I had received from some guy, she was always so sympathetic. She was constantly trying to convince me that I had to slow down and be careful with who I went out with. I pretended to listen and then went about my business, doing exactly what I wanted to do. I believed in living by the rule "you only live once." Besides, I was no dummy. I knew what all men wanted, and I was honest enough with myself to know that I won't have what they want forever. So, I had to find a man that would give me all the good things in life -- things that won't disappear and will increase in value, like jewelry, property, and shares of stock.

For my future career, I had decided to be a doctor, but I had only chosen that profession because when we had to do a report in high school of different occupations and the salaries they would bring, a doctor was at the top of the list. It would bring me respectability in the community and allow me access to other wealthy people. The next thing to do was decide what kind of doctor I would be. I really didn't like blood all that much and so becoming a surgeon was out. I didn't want anything to do with female parts, mainly because I found most women to be whiny and irritating. I had discovered that I couldn't tolerate my own gender very well. I settled on pediatrician. I wasn't crazy about kids, either, but with that type of practice, I knew I could keep pretty good hours, if I was able to join a pediatrician's group, and then I would only be on call once in a while. If the kids had contracted anything serious, I could send him or her to a specialist or surgeon. I figured looking down tonsils and into ear canals for infections and giving shots would be a pretty good job. And the money would be great. So I set my plans and goals for the future based on that. Of course, there would be a lot of studying and years of schooling, rotations, and interning ahead of me, but if it worked out like I had planned, it would all be worth it.

Kate had held her ground and had not gone to the frat party. I was glad in a way because things had gotten a little wilder than I had thought they would. I wasn't embarrassed by my behavior; I just didn't want her going to Mom and Dad with stories about me. I had plans to go to a new party this weekend, and it was quite a bit different than the others. I had been invited to a charity ball at the country club. One of the jocks I had met at a previous party wanted me to go with him to his parents' club, and he asked if I could find someone as beautiful as I was for his buddy. I told him I had a sister, and she was almost my equal, but not quite, and if his friend could handle that, I would ask her. So I was at Kate's dorm room once again, to ask her for a favor.

"Hey, Kate, what's up?"

"Oh, hi, Lily, I was just about to call you. I thought you might want to catch a movie and get pizza afterwards. I got my studying done, and I'm ready for some fresh air. I'm tired of looking at these same four walls." Kate looked at me expectantly with her big eyes. The little wimp just couldn't get enough of wanting to be with her twin.

"Sure, I'm up for that. But only if you agree to do a favor for me."

"Of course, Lily, anything, you know that."

"I want you to go on a blind date with Jason's friend, Derrick. We'll double-date so you won't feel so awkward. I'll be right there with you the whole time. Plus, it's a fancy country club dance, and we'll have a chance to dress up."

"Oh, Lily, you know I hate to go on blind dates. I prefer to know what kind of person he is first. I've had enough of the guys at this college. They all just want one thing. I'm tired of pushing hands away and having tongues stuck down my throat. Give a guy a little alcohol and he thinks you're his personal play toy."

"I actually agree with you on that one." I thought if I went along with her logic she might change her mind. I, personally, enjoyed being someone's play toy. "But honestly, Jason is one of the best guys I've met here, and he has manners to boot. I don't know Derrick very well, but I have hung out with him a few times. He seems like a real nice person and respectful, too. Besides both of them come from very good backgrounds, and they could do a lot for us in the future with all of their parents' connections."

Kate frowned a little at that last comment. I realized I might have gone a little too far. She didn't believe in looking for a mate in a calculating manner. She always said she wanted to marry for love no matter who the guy was or where he came from, which in my opinion, was so childish and very unrealistic. "But of course, that's not the point," I went on. "It would be fun to go to a party with some guys and act like grown-ups for a change. We have to practice on how to deal with the outside world. Once we graduate and the doors start to open for us, it would be nice to feel comfortable with how the other half lives."

"Well, all right. I guess a new experience couldn't hurt. But you'd better be right about this Derrick."

I gave her a hug, because I knew how she loved the sisterly thing. "Let's go, I'll let you pick the movie."

We actually had a good time that night, just the two of us. And later that week we went shopping for new makeup and hair products. Mom had sent us to college this year with one party dress each, just in case, and we hadn't worn them yet. So we were all set with our outfits.

On Saturday night the guys picked us up right on time. Kate was a little shy, but she seemed to warm up to Derrick quickly after that. I could tell he liked the idea of being with a look-alike-me. Guys were so predictable. No doubt they would compare notes later to see who had the hottest twin. I'd make sure I would win that conversation. Jason knew exactly what he would be getting when we were alone later.

About half-way through the evening, I looked around for Kate and Derrick and didn't see them anywhere. The last time I saw them together, they were dancing very close to a slow song. Kate's eyes were closed as he moved her around the dance floor. It looked like love was in the air. "Jason, have you seen the two love birds?"

"They stepped out for some fresh air. How about you and I do the same? I know a nice cozy corner in the gardens. It's very private; I've been waiting to get you alone all night."

Just as we stepped outside, I saw Kate. She was crying and her hair was a mess. Derrick was nowhere around but another boy was with her, holding her up with his arm around her waist.

"Kate, what's wrong?" I ran over to her and noticed that the spaghetti strap on her dress was torn loose.

"It seems that Derrick isn't the gentleman he pretended to be. He kept saying, 'you know you want it, baby. Your sister always does.' What in the world did you tell him about me? If it wasn't for David, here, I don't know what I would have done. I couldn't fight him off anymore."

"And who is David, and how does he fit into this picture?"

Then the most handsome guy I had ever seen on campus stepped forward with his hand outstretched. "I'm David Smith. My mother is the chairperson for this event. She always has to force me to come, but tonight I'm very glad I was here. Kate was in real trouble when I came along. Let's just say, Derrick will have a story to tell when he explains his fat lip."

"Nice to meet you David. Thank you so much for stepping in like that. Are you all right, Kate?" I did a quick once over of Kate's appearance; she looked fine other than a little dirt on her face and some smeared lipstick.

"I'm okay, really, but if you don't mind I'm going home now. David said he would get me a cab, so you two can stay."

"Are you sure? We can take you home."

"No, it's okay. You were so looking forward to tonight; I don't want to ruin your evening. I'll be fine."

"Okay, if you insist. I'll check in on you later."

And that was the beginning of Kate and David. He was instantly drawn to her. It must have been that his hero complex was satisfied when he saved a 'damsel in distress.' I don't know what else he would have seen in Kate. She was definitely out of his league. David, it turned out, was a real good catch. His parents were both physicians, and held a lot of sway in the community. Suddenly David was looking real good, besides being good looking. I decided to wait a little while before I made my move. He wouldn't know what hit him.

⌘ Chapter Eighteen ⌘

Kate ~ 2014

"From the time we were very young, my sister Lily would tell me that she was the beautiful one. She always followed that comment with a sympathetic, 'I'm so sorry for you. It must be terrible to be my twin. I can't help it if the boys like me best – really.' I knew early on what the boys liked best about her, and it had more to do with what she was willing to give to them than what she looked like."

Conor reached for my hand and said, "Before you go any further, I want to say that you are beautiful, one of the most beautiful women I have ever seen, and I hope you know it."

"I've been told that I am pretty, but the years with Lily did a number on my self-esteem, and it's been very difficult to overcome. She worked her magic on my high school boyfriend and ended up going to the prom with him. I did get another date, just not the one I wanted. And then came college."

I paused to begin clearing dishes and Conor jumped up to help, motioning that I should continue talking while we worked. "David Smith was the love of my life. He was pre-med while I was going for my library of science degree. As soon as he met Lily, I could see the sparks fly, but I was older now and knew how to keep her in line. Lily's interest was short-lived, as usual, and she went on to chasing someone else, and soon she was too busy in her own pre-med studies to be around David and me. She had some classes with David but at that point I wasn't worried. I knew he loved me, after all he had proposed, and we had promised each other a wonderful life once he graduated and became a doctor. We laughed at the fact that my name would be Kate Smith, the same as another of Daddy's favorite singers. Those years were hard but we made it through, both of us working long hours in our careers as we struggled to pay back college loans. We were married as soon as he found a position with a well-respected general practitioner. Of course, Lily was my maid of honor. It was what we had always planned, on the days we were getting along, and, of course, mother expected it. I thought I caught a little flirtation between David and Lily at the wedding reception, and maybe the congratulatory kiss and hug was a bit longer than it should have been, but I chalked it off to too much wine. I was high on life and didn't think anything could interfere with my fairy tale."

Conor said, "I can almost see where this is going. Let's go sit on the sofa in front of the fire." He stroked my cheek tenderly with his knuckles and we sat facing each other, holding hands like children.

"Lily went off to start her career in New Mexico, and I was actually happy that she was so far away. As it turned out, she was a brilliant doctor, and everyone seemed to love her. David and I continued on with our lives, and soon we began to want a family. We dreamed of children who would look just like us. I imagined kissing away scraped knees and receiving tight hugs with fat little arms. We tried and tried but nothing ever happened. We weren't to the point yet of making charts of cycles and temperatures; I didn't want to kill the romance. We were really hoping it would happen naturally."

Somehow Conor had gently moved me around so I was leaning back against his chest with his arms around me. I felt completely safe with this man, and so I continued on, baring my soul. "Then a few years ago, my mother got sick. Daddy had passed away the year before; so this was an exceptionally tough time. Lily flew back and forth as often as she could; I took time off from the library so I could spend her last days with her here in River County. Then eventually the inevitable happened and there were so many arrangements to be made. The burden was on me, because both David and Lily had their practices. Somehow we made it through the service and burial, and the small reception we held here at the lodge. Finally the last guests were gone, and I realized that both Lily and David were missing. I thought they were outside on the porch saying goodbye to a lingering guest. I was exhausted, grieving, and had a splitting headache, so I climbed the stairs to go lay down for a few minutes."

I paused here to catch my breath, because I realized I had been talking faster and faster as if I had no choice but to get it all out quickly. I slowed my speech pattern down and forged ahead. "You've probably guessed that I walked in on them, in my mother's bedroom of all places; they were kissing passionately. Lily had her leg up and around David's thigh and he had his hand up her skirt. Her blouse was already half off. They didn't even try to conceal their moans and sighs, or maybe they had just totally forgotten where they were. I'll still never understand why they had to have each other in Mama's bedroom on the day of her burial. To me it was the ultimate betrayal. Lily must have heard my sharp intake of breath, and realized I was there. Instead of being embarrassed, she just tossed her hair, looked over David's shoulder, and gave me her sly grin, as if to say, I finally got your man. There was lots of crying, yelling, and I have to admit, hysterics. When I demanded an explanation, they both confirmed that they had been in love for quite some time, as if that made it all okay. I didn't stick around long enough to

227

find out how long they had been having their affair, or when and where they had been meeting; maybe it had been going on since college. I guess I'll never know the extent of it and I still don't understand why David consented to try to have a child with me. Suddenly, I couldn't deal with it anymore, so I ran out, got in my car, and drove and drove." My voice began to get shaky, and I had to stop.

Conor was now rubbing my arm and kissing me on the top of the head.

"I can't imagine how awful that must have been for you," he said. "I take it you divorced, then?"

"Yes, I went straight to a lawyer. With no children, it was over in a matter of weeks and before long I was back to being Kate Lemanski again. I was still reeling from it all when the battle over the house began. I had no choice but to see them at the reading of the will. We didn't speak or acknowledge each other in any way. The property was left to both of us, equally, in the will. I think our parents had thought we would time-share or something so the lodge would stay in the family and be passed on to the next generation. I wanted to keep the house, but Lily wanted to sell it. She never did have an appreciation of this area. So we decided I would buy out her half, and because of the poor housing market, there was a big disagreement on the value. We've had our lawyers fighting it out for the past three years. I finally gave up and paid her what she wanted just to get her off my back. Through it all, I was a basket of nerves. I lost a lot of weight, and my friends were worried about my health, both mentally and physically. I had decided after that, for my own well-being, I would never speak to Lily and David again.

"During that three year time period, she married David. He had set up his practice in Albuquerque, in order to be near her already thriving practice. So I felt safe that I would never have to be around them ever again. I was just getting ready to come out here to get a new start on life, when I got a call from Lily. I almost didn't take the call, but at the last second, I picked up. She was my sister, after all, and maybe there was an emergency or something had happened to David. Instead, she was all happy and bubbly as if nothing had ever come between us. She wanted me to know that she was carrying David's child – the one I was unable to give him. All I ever wanted in life was to be a wife and mother, and she had taken both chances from me. I honestly don't know if she realized how much that hurt. Could she really be that cruel to me on purpose? Her own twin sister? The answer of course, is yes. Deep in my heart, I know that now, and I finally see Lily for who she really is."

Exhausted after the telling, I went limp in Conor's arms and sobbed. He gently turned me around and kissed my tears. He held me for a long time until I realized where I was and what I had just revealed to this man I really didn't know all that well yet.

"I must look a mess," I said now feeling embarrassed at my outpouring of emotions.

"I'm so sorry. It's only our first real date, and here I am blubbering in your arms." I could barely look him in the eyes.

"Never worry about your feelings when you're

around me. Besides what you felt was perfectly natural. Your sister doesn't seem like a very moral person, or maybe she just has some mental issues. I hope she's a better surgeon than she is a sibling. I don't know David, but there's no excuse for the way he behaved. In my book, and almost everyone I know, David would not be thought of as much of a man."

I walked over to the sink to splash a little water on my face. I needed to change the subject, or he would always think of me in this way. Desperate and needy. I turned to him, smiled weakly and said, "I'd like to forget it all for the moment, if you don't mind. Let's not end this night on a depressing or sad note. Besides there is something else I have to talk to you about, anyway. Let's have another glass of wine."

He furrowed his eyebrows and tilted his head inquisitively. "This sounds serious, too." He held up his glass. "Pour."

⌘ Chapter Nineteen ⌘

Kate ~ 2014

We filled our glasses with wine, and this time Conor sat opposite me, in the big overstuffed chair near the hearth. He leaned forward with his arms on his knees, hands linked, looking at me intently. I slowly walked over to the records and CDs, knowing that music can set a mood like no other. I needed something long-playing so we would not be interrupted when it clicked off. I wasn't sure how he felt about classical music, but I decided to select some chamber music from St. Martin-in-the Fields. It should be just perfect for a quiet background sound.

"Well," he smiled. "You really are diverse with your music tastes, aren't you?"

"Is it okay? I was raised to love music of all genres."

"Fine, by me. I actually appreciate any music, as long as it's good."

"Wonderful," I said. "Now where to begin?"

"At the beginning?" he asked.

"It's a long way back but I'll give it a try. While cleaning my mother's closets, I discovered a letter from my grandmother addressed to me. She asked a favor of me, and left behind some information so I could look into it after her death. It actually involves you – or your family, anyway."

"Really?" He looked quite puzzled. He leaned forward even more, and I saw his body tense with anticipation.

"I think the simplest way would be for you to read the letters yourself, or I can read it to you. There's a letter explaining what my grandmother wanted me to do, and then there's a journal that tells the story."

"I love being read to," he said. "Would you read it aloud, please, Kate?" He relaxed a little and sat back in his chair.

And so I began. I read on and on. At one point Conor got up and stoked the fire in the fireplace. I glanced up throughout the narrative and watched his body language. He was taking in every word, but I wasn't sure how he was "taking" it exactly. When I had finished the journal, I looked up at him.

"That's quite a story," he said thoughtfully. "My mind is swimming with the facts. In plain language, what does that mean? And more importantly, how does it affect us?"

I let out a big sigh. I needed to find the right words so it would be understandable to someone who was just hearing this for the first time, and did not have a professional grasp on genealogy. "In plain language, Jamie is your grandfather's son, therefore your father's half-brother. That makes him your uncle."

"Okay, I get that," he said slowly. "Now, go over your family line again so I can understand how he connects to you."

"He's a little farther removed from me. Jamie is my grandmother's nephew, through her sister Hattie. That means that Jamie is my mother's cousin, and so my second cousin." I started to shake as I realized this might be enough to turn Conor away from me. It was then that I realized how much this kind and gentle man meant to me. It had only been a short time since we had met here at the lodge when he came to return my house key and rocked my world; I think the feelings were elevated quickly because of our first encounter and kiss when we were teens. I had not anticipated falling for someone just yet, but Conor has been the salve on my wounds, and at this moment he seemed to be my lifeline. If he turned from me now, I don't know how I would handle it.

Conor stood slowly with his back toward me. When he turned to look at me, his brow was furrowed. There was a slight pause that seemed to last for a lifetime, and then he grinned and clapped his hands together. "Well, this is going to make an interesting story to tell in the future. I think we can deal with it, Miss Lemanski!"

I rose and went to him. We wrapped our arms around each other. The kiss was slow and sweet. A warmth spread all the way through me and went straight to my heart. At that moment, it felt like all was right in the world.

Conor said a little breathlessly, "Hmm, your lips feel very familiar. I've tasted them in my dreams for many years."

"And I've tasted yours, Jack!" And we both burst out laughing.

After a few luscious minutes, we pulled away from each other. Conor looked into my eyes and with a serious tone, asked, "So, what's next?"

"I do have a little more I haven't shared with you yet." I handed him the obituary I had discovered just a few days ago. "I'm very sorry to show you that. I was so hoping we could meet him."

"Me, too," he said. "I'm going to have to tell all of this to my dad and Aunt Cindy. I'm sure they don't know they had a half-brother. I wonder how Aunt Cindy will feel about her childhood sweetheart actually being her brother?"

"Yes, you'll have to tread lightly with that bit of information, since we have no idea how far it went."

Conor still held the obituary in his hand. "Can I show this to Dad?"

"Of course," I said reaching into the drawer of the end table behind me. "I ran copies of everything for you. Let him read them at his own pace, and if he doesn't understand anything or has any questions at all, please call me. Feel free to pass this around your family. Ellen should know, too. It's all about your heritage as well as mine."

"Thank you, Kate. It's been a wonderful evening in so many ways, and at the same time a little unsettling, if you know what I mean, so I think I'd better be going. I need to digest this and find the right words to tell my father."

"I do know what you mean, and of course, I understand completely." I took his hand in mine, and said, "Just, please, don't be a stranger."

"Oh, Kate, we will never be strangers again, now that we know we're family." His teasing smile showed me that he was not going to let this news interfere with our relationship. I felt like I was floating, because no matter what, I just knew he would always be in my life.

⌘ Chapter Twenty ⌘

Kate ~ 2014

I didn't sleep much Friday night. There was a lot of tossing and turning and tangling in the sheets. Images of Sophie, Hattie, Ryan, and Jamie kept going round and round in my head. I had missed out on the chance for more detailed interviews with them; Jamie had passed away before I was born, and the others probably weren't ready to reveal their side of the story anyway when I was old enough to ask. Now they were all gone, and we would never hear the story directly from those who knew it best. So other than my grandmother's writings, which were based on a little girl's observations, it was mostly speculation now.

I decided to call Cara before going to bed. I knew she was a night owl, and with the time difference, it was safe to call. I told her the whole story, and expressed my concerns about my relationship with Conor. As always, Cara had a no-

nonsense, clearheaded approach to my dilemma. Even though she can come off as being a little ditsy and flighty at times, she has an uncanny ability to see straight through a problem; she always centers me and calms me in times of trouble. Her advice? Let love take its own course. Don't try to force it. If it's meant to be, it's meant to be. And then, just like Mama, she actually said, Que Sera Sera. I took that as a sign and decided to heed her advice.

     I made a decision to give Conor and his family some time and space, so I didn't call or text. He would come to me when he was ready. I knew his father, Eric, had an illness; I had never inquired about what it was, but maybe Conor had to tell the story in such a way that it would not upset his recovery. Saturday morning was dark and dreary. The clouds looked ominous and the air felt heavy. I took Hoagy out for a short walk in the woods before the inevitable downpour began. The smell of fresh water was in the air, sweeping in moisture from Lake Michigan, even this far inland. The impending storm was going to be a doozy. We had just come back in and closed the lodge door when the first clap of thunder rang out. There's nothing like a thunderstorm in the woods. It echoes throughout miles of woodlands and seems to be ten times louder than in the city. The wind began to build up speed, and I heard a loose limb fall to the ground with a thud. It sounded like a cannon going off, vibrating the floor that I stood on.

I hated to let anyone know it, but I am terrified of storms. A loud thunder-boom, as we called them when we were kids, is always jarring, but the electric display of lightening can put me right under the bed. I went around the house gathering up candles just in case the power went out, trying to be brave and act like a grownup. Hoagy and I sat in the middle of the room, just in case a tree came through a window. He sat right on my feet, sensing my fear. It was that bad! And then just as fast as it had come in, it left. I could hear the thunder rumbling miles away as it moved quickly on its path. I opened the door to see if there was any major damage out there. Nothing much but a few overturned lightweight chairs. A garden basket I had left out had blown across the yard, and a birdfeeder had fallen to the ground.

Suddenly, the sun peeked through, slowly at first, and then as soon as it found a hole in the clouds, it burst forth in full glory. The birds instantly took notice and began to sing, announcing to all of their feathered friends that they had made it through the violent activity. I pulled on my still beautiful, red boots, and Hoagy and I walked out to smell the wonderful fresh air, which was now fully charged with ozone. The puddles had receded quickly into the sodden ground and my garden plants looked greener than ever before, their leaves standing up at attention, reaching for light. I decided to wait a bit and then come back out in a few hours and continue to pull weeds and move plants. Many of them would need to be divided and replanted, while others had to be discarded. It would be a big, and now muddy, job, but one I looked forward to.

Several hours later, after I had had a much needed shower and cup of coffee followed by a light brunch, there was a firm knock on the door. I only knew a few people, so it must be either Conor or Ellen. I held my breath and walked slowly, not knowing what was waiting for me on the other side. It was Conor, mussed hair, unshaven, excited as a little boy, but looking like a Greek god to me.

"Kate, I'm so glad you're okay. That was a pretty wicked storm," he said, while taking me in his arms. "I was going to call first, but I had to come and see you right away."

"Yes, I'm fine – now. I have to admit to not liking storms much. But it looks like you have something else on your mind. What's up? How did it go with your Dad and Cindy? What did Ellen think? Come in, sit, and tell me everything!"

I poured him some coffee and we took our usual seats at the table, already falling into a pattern of a couple who had known each other for a long time. Conor placed some papers face down in front of him. I could see that he was anxious to talk about them.

"I couldn't sleep" he began, "so I started to

think about everything we talked about. We are the fourth generation in our house, too, the same as you. I knew there were plenty of boxes in the attic, but I had never been interested in the past before, so I had never had any curiosity about what was in the old trunks and boxes. I tiptoed up to the attic and spent the night going through everything I could find that looked old. I discovered something you will find very interesting. But first I wanted to tell my Dad everything we knew so far, and get his permission to show you. I told him I wanted to invite Aunt Cindy to join us for breakfast."

"How did he take the news that he had a brother he knew nothing about?"

"He was shocked, of course, and then angry. But after I went over the details with him and Aunt Cindy, we all came to see that it was more a product of the times – an era of family secrets. In the forties and fifties, perception was everything. They always wanted their neighbors and friends to think they had a perfect life; dirty laundry was never aired. Privacy was cherished. Basically, it was just the way things were then. We talked about visiting Jamie's gravesite, when the weather is better and Dad is up to it. He has severe arthritis that gets him down at times, so we'll have to wait for one of his good days, and then we'll take a ride to the Traverse area. Dad wants to meet you, and has invited you to Sunday dinner tomorrow. He's very grateful for all you have done, and holds nothing against your family."

"That's very kind," I said. "I look forward to seeing the man who raised a son like you. I accept the invitation. And I'm thankful there will be no hard feelings between us. We wouldn't want to start a Hatfield and McCoy war." I smiled and placed my hand over his. He gripped it tightly.

"We could not, in good conscience, ever fault your family for any wrong doing, because it seems there was a cover-up in our family, also." And with that he pushed his small packet of papers toward me. "I found these in my great-grandmother's trunk inside a box marked Ryan. It included his discharge papers, and newspaper clippings of some of the action his unit saw in World War II. It looks like he was in the worst of it, but then I suppose most men were. Buried in the bottom were these letters."

There were three letters, each one addressed to Hattie Bauer, in care of Mr. and Mrs. Andrew McAuley, Conor's great-grandparents. You could tell they had been opened a long time ago. I hesitated, and then with an encouraging nod from Conor, I turned the first one over, pulled out a thin sheet of airmail paper, and began to read.

My sweet, sweet, Hattie,

I'm writing to you at my parents' address because I'm not sure if you have told your folks about us yet. I didn't want to cause any problems. In a separate letter I asked Mom to give this to you without anyone knowing. I just have a few minutes before lights out so I'll just write a short note. I'm here at base at Fort Benning Georgia, waiting for our orders to go overseas. Sarge thinks we'll be leaving real soon. I'm not sure when I'll be allowed to write again, so I wanted to tell you how I feel about what happened between us before I left. I never meant for it to happen, but I just needed your love so much. If I was home, I would marry you in a minute to preserve your honor. Please don't think that I have ruined your reputation. No one needs to know but us. I know I am almost five years older than you, and I feel terrible that we made love when you were so young and inexperienced. But I knew you wanted it too, didn't you? When I get home, I'll make an honest woman out of you, I promise. I hope this war doesn't last too long so we can be together once more.

> Your loving jitterbug partner,
> Ryan

Darling Hattie,

I sure hope you got my last letter. I would love to hear from you. You can always send something to the return address on the envelope. The Army will find a way to forward mail to us whenever we are at camp and have a few days' break. I understand from some of the fellas, that it is rough here. I haven't seen any action yet, though.

Oh, by the way, I forgot to say, I am no longer in the States. I'm already in ---------------------- .

I looked up from the page. "It's all blacked out."

"Yeah, I saw that too," said Conor. "I understand that someone had to read all of the letters before they were sent home, to make sure the location and movement of the troops were not disclosed. I guess he said something there that was considered classified."

After skipping the blackened section, there wasn't much left to read. It ended saying:

I'm sending home my pay for my parents to keep for us. I don't need much, just enough for my cigarettes. And I don't plan on gambling it away like some of the guys do. So we should have a good nest egg to start our new life together. I dream of your sweet face every night,

All my love, Ryan

"He loved her," I said quietly. "It wasn't a case of a guy wanting to satisfy his own needs before he went off to war. He wanted to come home to her and get married. It's not what I expected at all."

Conor smiled ruefully. "Keep reading. You might be able to glean even more of the story."

"Okay. Next letter."

My Dearest Hattie,

I wish I knew if any of this was reaching you. I trusted my mother to deliver my letters. I know she must feel you are too young for me, but she promised me she would follow my instructions. All I can do, is hope you are reading this and are just afraid to answer for fear your parents would find out. It's really tough here, but I won't tell you about it until I get home. I don't want to worry you. At least there's one good thing. I'm not like some of the guys who have to walk everywhere we go. I was lucky enough to be trained as a radioman, so I most often ride in a Jeep with the equipment. I'll be all right, really I will. And every night that I can see the sky – some nights are too thick with smoke from the bombs – I look at the moon at 10:00 p.m. and think about you, just like we said we would do. Knowing you are doing the same, makes me feel closer to home and especially to you. I pray for you daily, and I'm sure you are praying for me, too. I can feel it all the way across the ocean. Take care of your sweet self, I'll be home soon, little jitterbug.

Love forever, Ryan

"How wonderfully romantic," I said, with tears in my eyes. "But so sad also. I don't think Hattie ever knew he wrote to her, and probably never knew how deep his feelings went."

Conor added, "That's what I meant by secrets on my side of the family. It looks like my great-grandmother held these letters and never let Hattie know that her son loved her. I guess she thought she was doing what was best for her son, or maybe she had someone else in mind for him to marry. Either way, she interfered in their lives, and it changed the course of history for so many people."

"And, of course, we'll never know what she would have done had she known that Hattie was pregnant with her son's child," I said. "And if she ever had found out, how would she explain that she had kept the letters away from her on purpose? I'm now wondering if Hattie would have agreed to give her son to her mother if she knew the man she loved was coming home to her. Maybe they would have married and then Jamie's life, too, would have been completely different."

Conor gnawed his lip, thinking. "Apparently, no one ever let their secrets out, or my great-grandparents and yours would not have remained friends. I wonder what happened when Ryan came home."

"He must have been heart-broken to find Hattie had married someone else and moved away." I shook my head in disbelief. "I know when many soldiers returned, they found that their girls had fallen in love with someone else while they were gone. But it doesn't sound like Ryan had even given that a thought. He truly thought she would be waiting for him. How absolutely awful! I don't even know what to say."

"I feel the same, but at this point, there's nothing we can do to change a thing."

"Yes, I know," I said. "You're absolutely right. I do have one request, though. When you go to Jamie's gravesite, I'd like to come. Will your father agree to it?"

"I'm sure he will. He's really quite a guy. I think you're going to like him, and I'm sure he'll like you, too. Speaking of my father, I'd better get back home. I'll see you tomorrow at noon for dinner?"

"You sure will. I'll walk through the woods if it's nice. Let me walk you out a ways; I'm not quite ready to let you go yet."

We wrapped our arms around each other's waists and then went as far as the bent pine. We sat for a few minutes on the lawn swing nearby which hung from a log A-frame. We looked into each other's eyes, now knowing that there was more to that first meeting as teens that had been linking us together. Conor reached inside his jacket pocket, pulled out a red envelope, and handed it to me.

"I was going to give this to you tomorrow, but I think I'd rather have you read it in private instead of in front of the family."

"It looks like a Valentine," I said with a laugh. "Aren't we a little late in the year for that?"

"You'll see."

Inside of the large red envelope was a very beautiful Valentine. It was frilly and very French. The heading read 'Joyeuse Saint Valentin, mon amour', or Happy Valentine Day, my love, and then in Ryan's handwriting:

"I found these words chiseled into a cornerstone on a building. They seemed just right for you and me. 'As a body everyone is single, as a soul never.' Hermann Hesse, 1927. Hattie, You are my soul mate, and we can never be parted.

I love you, Ryan

"That's so beautiful," I said.

"I agree," Conor nodded. "I want you to have it. It's exactly how I feel about us. I think we were meant to be together, Kate. And even though the lives of our ancestors were so tangled up with their own lies and deceit, it was because of those very acts that we are here today. If Ryan had married Hattie instead of Roma, they would not have produced my father, and I would not be alive. Your life would probably not be much different, but because our parents remained friends, we were connected from the start, and I was then trusted to watch over your house. You came here for a reason, Kate, and it was for more than learning to get over your past. It was to find your future – with me, I hope."

"I think you're right. I know it, in fact. You and I will never be a single body again. Like Ryan and Hattie, I feel as if we, too, are soul mates."

We sat together in silence, swinging gently back and forth and looking past the bent pine, down the embankment to the river. The water was moving slowly now, as if it knew it was time to settle into the new routine of summer. Life was ever changing just like the seasons, and, like the river, I was about to begin the next season of my life. I said a silent prayer – thanking God and great-grandma Sophie, for guiding my way through the tangled roots of Bent Pine Lodge. Maybe soon I'll feel whole again, and be able to forget the wrongs which have been done to me. Then and only then will I be able to forgive, and with any luck, Conor will be at my side.

The weak can never forgive.

Forgiveness is the attribute of the strong.

Mahatma Gandhi

The White Pine Trilogy

Book Two

The Dunes & Don'ts

Antiques Emporium

⌘ Chapter One:

Audrey Doane ⌘

Audrey turned the key to the door of her shop, The Dunes and Don'ts Antiques Emporium, the same as she did every morning at 9:30. She loved entering through the front so she could get the same effect that her customers got when they came in. There was a time when the creak of the old door and the jingling of the bell was so exciting she could hardly wait to get started with her day, because being the owner of her very own business had satisfied a lifelong dream, but lately a strange feeling had overcome her and it just would not go away. It was a heavy, dark, feeling of loneliness and despair; it felt as if there was a bag of cement sitting on her back and she had to carry it with her wherever she went, and it was exhausting!

Depression was unknown to Audrey. She was usually positive and happy all the time. It was this same sparkling personality that had gotten her this far in life, and she had done it all on her own, with not one lick of help from anyone. She was proud of that. Audrey had had to scrape and fight for everything she had ever achieved; she knew how to overcome adversity. So why now, she wondered. Why couldn't she get over this awful feeling? She had everything she ever wanted, didn't she? What was missing?

Oh well, she would just put on a pleasant face for the customers; besides no one ever seemed to notice when she was faking it. Maybe that was part of the problem. Not one person ever noticed! She took a deep breath inhaling and exhaling slowly, just like she had been taught at yoga class. It actually did help quite a bit. She felt a little better, enough to get through the day, anyway. Maybe she would be able to push aside the warnings of impending doom for one more day. She forced a smile, just to try it out, and pinched her cheeks to add a little more color. "I need to be upbeat and ready for the new day. The show must go on," she said to herself.

Once her day began and she was busy with the routine chores, she forgot all about her problems, or whatever they were. She turned on all of the lights, even the crystal chandeliers hanging overhead, making her shop sparkle with visions of an era gone by, when life was gentle, slower paced, and everyone knew exactly what was expected of them. Now it seemed a person no longer knew how they were supposed to act, or what they were supposed to wear to any kind of function including a funeral or a baby shower, or just to go visit with a friend for an afternoon. "Jeans!" Audrey said out loud with disgust, "doesn't anyone own anything else?"

Sometimes, people looked at Audrey as if she was from another era. The fifties-style shirtwaist dresses found at thrift shops fit her trim figure perfectly, accentuating her curves in all the right places. She loved the lower heeled shoes, raising her up just two inches, giving her calf a shapely look without displaying a bulging muscle. The proper way she carried herself, standing straight and tall, looking everyone in the eye, showed everyone that she was a lady; which was exactly the image she had carefully created over the years. She was always mindful never to raise her voice, and her manners were impeccable at all times.

Years ago, when there was no one around to teach her the do's and don'ts of society, she had purchased an antique copy of Emily Post's book called Etiquette which was first printed in 1922. Since then it had become Audrey's bible. It might seem that, like the book, she, too, was born in the 1920s, but in fact, she was just an old soul. Audrey was actually the ripe old age of 39, and the dreaded number 40 was just around the corner. Lately, just the thought of the number forty could send Audrey into a tearful shudder, dabbing gently at her tears with her hankie, of course, so as not to redden her eyes. She wouldn't want the customers to see that she was in distress. That wouldn't be good for business.

Until last month, when she had had her 39th birthday, all was well. Audrey was very pleased with the life she had created for herself. A real sense of accomplishment came over her when she thought about how she had struggled to get this shop up and running, but she had done it! And to date, it seemed to be quite a success, and that pleased her very much. But one of her regular customers had teased her about the big 4-0 coming up next and that was when it hit her. She only had 11 months left to be in the young woman category! And then of course the soul-searching had begun about what life was all about and whether or not she had truly done anything worthwhile since she had been born.

All of these thoughts were swirling around in Audrey's head this morning, as she dusted and swept the floors before she unlocked the doors for the public and flipped over the Open sign. Audrey was often asked about the name of her store and how she had come to name it the Dunes and Don'ts. She then told the story about when she was in school in the first grade. She had done something wrong and the teacher said, "Don't you know you shouldn't be doing that?" And she had replied with, "I'm sorry. I don't know all the dunes and Doanes yet." Growing up on the shores of Lake Michigan, she had heard the word as 'dunes' and she had misunderstood 'don't' for Doane, her last name. The teacher had burst out laughing, and she remembered feeling humiliated in front of everyone in class. It was the first thing that came to mind when the time came for naming her store, as she stood on her front porch looking out at the huge dune on the other side of the channel, but she decided to spell Doane so it could be easily read and understood – and that's how The Dunes and Don'ts Antiques Emporium was born.

Her shop was not large, nothing like one of those antiques malls, but Audrey had plenty of inventory and there was always something to dust. Old things needed a lot of attention. And then of course, they had to be inspected regularly for small chips, scratches, and lost price tags, which happened often after the customers handled the merchandise. Audrey had purposely decided not to overcrowd her shop, like some of the other stores had done down the street; but preferring instead to leave the aisles wide, allowing for more elbow room when one browsing customer was passing another. It had prevented many a mishap, and she thought it also gave a classier feeling to her store. She was fussy with what she sold, too. None of that garage sale junk. Each and every item had to be at least 40 years old, and it must have a label or be from a well-known manufacturer so she could prove its age and therefore determine its true value. And there was that number forty again! Now even her antiques were making her feel old! Why, she realized, some of them were the same age she was. How had that happened? She decided maybe she should change the age rule of her antiques to 50 or even 70 years old. That would make her feel a little younger. Technically, true antiques were 100 years old, anyway; all the rest were considered collectibles. She didn't want to be known as only a collectibles shop, so maybe from now on her rule would be that every item must be 100 years old. There, that was a long way from 40. She felt much better now as she straightened her shoulders and got back to work.

The building housing The Dunes and Don'ts Antiques Emporium was actually a Sears Craftsman kit home built in the 1930s. It served double duty as the shop and also Audrey's home. A row of similar houses had been built along the shore of Lake Michigan in Fox Hill, and in recent years, most had been converted to gift and antiques shops catering to the booming tourist business which had been great for the community. Audrey had always planned to buy her own antiques shop someday, and eventually she had saved a small nest egg. So when this four bedroom Craftsman came on the market, she just knew she had to have it. Her vision was clear. The living room and dining room would be perfect for the store for starters; she could expand later when she had more money by opening up one wall of the living room to the front bedroom. As long as she kept the entrance to the kitchen through the dining room locked, she would be safe and secure in her living quarters. The wide front porch with its brick columns was perfect for putting out a few weathered antiques and on one side she would have a porch swing for her customers to use, but also for her own use after hours.

Audrey had perfect credit and a sizable down payment. The sale went through quickly and smoothly. She had been buying antiques at garage sales, auctions, and online for several years, and had them packed away in a storage unit, since her apartment had been too small for the many boxes she had accumulated. She'd had to hire painters, electricians, and plumbers to make sure everything was up to code, and as soon as the house passed inspection, she was granted her business license by the Fox Hill City Council. That was three years ago, and Audrey thought that might have been the happiest day in her life.

Audrey had a large group of friends and acquaintances, and she had had to call on every single one of them for help in one way or another. Shelves had to be assembled, and large pieces of furniture needed to be moved in. There was a

board, a curved glass secretary, two heavy oak
cher/library desks, and the oak counter she had
irchased at an auction from a dime-store that had
nally gone out of business after 75 years. She was
even lucky enough to be the one to buy their cash
register. The bidding had been fierce, but then so
had she. After moving day was over, and Audrey had
promised all of her friends a barbecue picnic in her
new back yard, she had collapsed with exhaustion
and slept soundly in her new upstairs bedroom. It
had been a little early in the year to open the
windows but she did anyway, just a crack, so she
could listen to the waves gently lapping at the shore.

The doorbell jingled, shaking Audrey out of
her reverie. Her first customer of the day had just
walked in.

"Good morning," she said with her usual
bright smile. "Are you looking for anything in
particular today?"